GOD'S
Frying Pan

Thanks for your support; Enjoy!

B.A. MAY

ISBN 978-1-0980-8637-4 (paperback)
ISBN 978-1-0980-8638-1 (digital)

Copyright © 2021 by B.A. May

All rights reserved. No part of this publication may be reproduced, distributed, or transmitted in any form or by any means, including photocopying, recording, or other electronic or mechanical methods without the prior written permission of the publisher. For permission requests, solicit the publisher via the address below.

Christian Faith Publishing, Inc.
832 Park Avenue
Meadville, PA 16335
www.christianfaithpublishing.com

Printed in the United States of America

PART 1

Life and Relationships

Chapter 1

A Theory

"I think God uses us as frying pans," Celia mused and put down her glass, as if for effect, while gazing off into the afternoon.

Gemma raised her eyebrows, not really surprised by her friend's thought. In the amount of time they had known each other, Celia never ceased to amaze Gemma with her peculiar views and thoughts on the world around her.

"Go on," she encouraged, interested to hear where this was going.

"Well…" Celia gave her a wide-eyed stare like she was about to share the secrets of the universe. Gemma found herself leaning forward just in case she missed something.

The two women were sitting on Celia's balcony in the late afternoon sun. It was hot and humid, and the dappled shade the trees offered was not making any difference to the heat.

The air was thick and still.

It didn't bother Gemma, however. Where they were sitting at the back of the house was elevated and surrounded by trees, so it felt private and forgotten for a moment—far away from the responsibilities of actual life.

It was always mentally pleasant visiting with her friend. Celia was a busy hairdresser with three girls and one boy and a wonderfully chaotic creative home. There were always "projects" happening around the house. Sometimes it was garden-based or container gardening at least, sometimes it was art, mediums like paint or clay, and sometimes they were in the kitchen baking, or just cooking some fantastic ethnic creation. Sometimes it was science. Gemma could never tell who exactly was ever involved in these projects. At times it seemed like all the children and Celia, other times it was just Celia and one of them. Sometimes it seemed like no one at all was actually involved, and these projects were self-sustaining. But the energy in her home was always uplifted and positive. Gemma felt her spirits lift as soon as she walked in the door.

Celia was so wonderfully capable; she took everything in stride and made everything look easy. Gemma's son Noah, was eight years old, and also loved being at Celia's house. He was inside with Celia's kids, and the balcony was the only place the two women could have a private uninterrupted conversation.

Gemma loved the break being at Celia's house as well. Besides being continually full of color, creativity, and life, she loved the conversations she had with Celia even more, always so inspired and honest—something Gemma had a hard time finding at this point in life. Who would have thought that by the time a woman reached her forties after a lifetime of building and retaining friendships, suddenly it would be so hard to make friends?

Today, they were rolling around their ideas of God and where he is in the world and life.

*****

Gemma never really felt safe discussing God after growing up in a strict Roman Catholic home, where she was taught to believe in a vengeful God. Her parents were devout. Pleasure and joy was frowned upon, and life was to be full of sacrifice and hardship in His name. Her father was a big, tall man with a giant booming voice, who would often raise his voice, and his hand to his family in his efforts to keep them respectful of the Lord and his authority. Her mother was just as fearful, with a quick slap across the face if either of her girls spoke out of turn or were asking questions that "shouldn't be asked."

Gemma was never comfortable with even thinking about God, or questioning their belief in Him in any way. Both her parents were liberal with the leather strap when she'd get too "disrespectful" and "mouthy" in her own search for God's place in her life. She was taught early that questioning religion and God in their home was straight from the devil. She didn't ever think it was the devil driving her curiosity, she just wanted to know. However, these things were to be accepted and not questioned. It was a terrifying, and then suffocating environment for an inquisitive child and left a bad taste in her mouth as she grew up, resentful at the lack of freedom in her parents' thinking as if just thinking about the reasons how and why things fitted into their life would send them all on a one way trip to hell, and it would be all her fault.

As a result of being unable to satisfy her curiosity or separate their family life from the church, she had turned away from the church and the community she was raised in and was grateful college had given her an excuse to leave the small Midwest town she was originally from. She had been back only once for her sister's wedding.

Neither of her parents believed in modern technology, so they didn't even have email addresses. Gemma spoke to them maybe a couple of times a year by phone. They had been so loud in their disapproval of her marriage to Scott, (not so much that she was marrying him, but that they did it in the city they had been living in, which was the halfway point between both hometowns). They didn't particularly approve of Scott's line of work, or her own career choice, or his family. They had never actually said anything, but they didn't have to. Gemma always felt like such a disappointment to them, especially with her mother's long sighs and disapproving attitude. Gemma honestly couldn't remember a time that she had experienced any sort of acceptance or praise, or validation from either of her parents. She didn't make much of an effort to stay in contact beyond Christmas and birthdays. There was no point.

However, in her years since graduation, and her own experience with love and marriage, and especially since the birth of her only child, Gemma found herself curious about God's place in her life once more. It is hard to do your own discovering when everyone is either ready to write you off as a member of the "God squad," or be ready to re-baptize you in the blink of an eye. She had come to a lot of her ideas on her own, through reading and occasional late-night conversations with Scott. More of "surely there must be a higher power who created all of this, and us, and guides us more than what we, as mere mortals, can see and do, and create" type of conversations.

Gemma always had her own ideas of this higher power, but never really had anyone to bounce the ideas off or talk them through with a curious but noncommittal approach. She wanted Noah to have an awareness of a higher power/God. She found herself silently praying but would catch herself and stop. She didn't know if she was doing it right, or even *how* to pray anymore!

*****

Celia took a breath. "Well..." She began collecting her thoughts as if she'd been thinking about this for a while but hadn't heard them spoken yet—and she loved a dramatic pause.

"Obviously, all this is a metaphor, but in thinking about this God thing (she was referring to their last conversation from a few months ago) and where He is in the world, our lives, the cosmos, and how He influences or speaks to us and ultimately uses us, I think the best way to think of His influence in our lives is that we are all His frying pans. He throws things on us and at us to cook, as it were, and it's up to us to learn how to control our own heat and decide how quickly or slowly to cook something, that ultimately His end goal for us is to have as much experience with all sorts of situations—or ingredients to cook—so that over time we become master chefs and intuitively know how fast or slow to cook what's given to us. Sometimes we still have problems cooking various things…we rush at it too quickly and burn them or don't stir it enough and things stick, but then we also have the things we have perfected and cook proficiently every time."

Gemma let that sink in.

"Huh," she replied. "I'd never thought of it like that before, but I like that idea."

Celia laughed. "Does that even make sense? I've been developing this theory for a while, but never have anyone to discuss it beyond a few minutes' worth with Greg."

Celia's own husband was the executive chef at one of the top hotels in town, and with four kids, they didn't have much time to kick around ideas of God together either.

"Yes," Gemma replied, understanding exactly what Celia meant in words and intention. "I get it."

She went on, "It's like He is continually teaching us through our experiences, which are the ingredients."

"Yes." Celia nodded. "Sometimes we just need to let things simmer, and not rush into responding to a situation. It's okay to let it do its own thing for a while and just keep an eye on it without being intrusive, but other times, it works best with a rapid boil, which are the situations that require direct, quick action so that it doesn't bubble out of control or burn."

Gemma laughed. "You mean he's actually making us *work* and have to pay attention to our experiences and development? Good and bad? I guess I always just presumed He just *gave* it all to us—and only the good." Gemma realized how silly that sounded once the words were out of her mouth. Why would she think God only ever gave us good stuff? Where did the bad stuff come from? She had never really thought about that. Why had she never thought about *that* before? All the "why me" moments she'd had recently flashed through her mind.

"Well, He does in a way." Celia momentarily looked thoughtful. "But not in the entitled 'here is a gift, you don't have to do anything to appreciate it' way, more in a 'here is something that will only mean as much as you decide it's worth so you better pay attention and work with it because it's totally worth it' kind of way."

Gemma let that process for a few moments. She liked this idea, but it went against everything she had previously presumed, thought, and believed about God's effect on her life. So where did everything she believed originally come from? She didn't remember anyone actually teaching her about how God *actually* is in your life. Or did they? She remembered being taught all the things He would be angry about. This frying pan idea made so much sense to her, but where did everything else she knew and had drummed into her over the years fit in? She didn't have any recollection of anyone actually spelling out *how* God made His presence felt in her life.

"I like this idea." She grinned at Celia. "But how are we supposed to know whether or not we should be letting something flash fry or simmer? I mean usually, it's not until later when you re-evaluate how something went that you realize you could have done it differently or sometimes—" She thought of her recent life, "as soon as the words are out of my mouth!" Gemma laughed, half to herself, thinking of the times she snapped back at someone (usually her husband or child) when she should have just let things simmer—or she had let things simmer when she really should have been turning the heat up.

"True," agreed Celia. "I do think, however, if we can give ourselves some space, even just a moment to evaluate what is happening instead of just reacting or speaking all the time, I think that is when God has a chance to guide us and let us authentically participate in the experience of what we are dealing with."

Gemma wasn't sure she actually wanted to fully experience so many moments. She had a pang of guilt and awareness that she just wanted to hurry up and get stuff out of the way so she didn't have to deal with it so often in her life.

Did that mean she was missing out on all these opportunities to be learning and growing?

Since leaving home, she had tried so hard to turn her back on church and God. But in the years since, she had experienced so many things that had proven to her that there was a higher power, divine grace, and a force greater than mankind, she *knew* it was there. But then, how *did* she know? It was something she never really questioned, she just knew.

But how did she know?

Gemma liked the frying pan idea. That was something she could relate to and understand. It fitted nicely in her ideas of spiritualism, and she could see how it affected her life.

Obviously, there had to be good and bad in someone's life. Gemma thought momentarily of how fortunate she had been in her life. So did that mean in applying the frying pan idea that she was good at dealing with stuff? She didn't think that would be right, she didn't like feeling superior to anyone. Or was she missing all these lessons?

She felt confused, stupid, and slightly irritated all at once and was relieved when Lily, Celia's eight-year-old, came outside holding her arm out.

"Mom, look." There were three bright red scratch marks just starting to bleed on her inner arm. "Hannah scratched me."

Right on cue, Hannah the six-year-old came out and slammed the sliding glass door. "She made me!" she yelled defiantly.

"I did not!" Lily yelled back.

Celia stood up. "Okay, girls, what actually happened?"

The girls started talking over each other, their voices getting louder and more indignant. Celia rolled her eyes at Gemma, who shrugged. Celia turned and put one hand on Lily's shoulder.

"Let's go and wash that," she said as she herded them inside. Gemma heard Hannah pleading her case and Lily protesting.

It was clear their time today was done—which was fine with her. Although she enjoyed her exploratory conversations with Celia, sometimes she just felt out of her depth and semi-annoyed by her friends' open questioning of everything.

Are you supposed to question everything in life? Can't we just leave some stuff alone? Even as Gemma thought that, she knew that was not the truth. Everything should be open for questioning. She was trying hard to teach Noah to trust his gut and question what he did not understand, to gain a better understanding.

Gemma looked at her watch. It was getting close to dinner time, and being Sunday, all the Monday preparations rushed into her head. It was really time for her to go anyway.

Gemma followed them in to round up her own son, which wasn't difficult—he was playing video games in the living room with Celia's twelve-year-old son Ronan and Lily's twin, Sophie. "Time to go, Noah."

"Aww, Mom, ten more minutes. I'm almost at the next level."

She thought about it—or pretended to—for a moment, watching

the game to make sure it wasn't something inappropriate for Noah. She knew it wouldn't have been, which is why she didn't check in the first place.

"Okay, but only for as long as it takes me to say goodbye to Celia."

"Okay, thanks, Mom."

Gemma said her goodbyes and made vague arrangements for their next get together. It was always a hodgepodge of ideas and trying to recall schedules and plans they'd had previously, both of them knowing it would probably be at least another month or so till they caught up again. She gave her friend a hug, collected Noah, and headed out.

On the way home, Gemma called Scott, her husband, to see if he had made it to the supermarket as promised after he had a "quick beer and brunch" with a buddy who was in town for the weekend. Scott didn't answer, which accelerated her mood instantly to next-level irritated. She knew his phone was within reach, if not in his hand at all times. Now she didn't know if she'd have to get to the supermarket to buy food for the week tonight or not.

Why does he do this? If he didn't want to help, why would he say he'd do it? She simultaneously started thinking of what they did have in the fridge and pantry and whether or not she could get by with *not* going to the store this evening and how much time she had until Noah had to get to bed and what they could have for dinner. Her head swam, thoughts charging in and pushing away any tranquility she had gained from being at Celia's.

I bet he's drunk and freaking clueless right now. Gemma couldn't help but let the negative thoughts creep in. Scott was always most concerned with Scott's good time. This personality trait had really raised its selfish head recently.

*****

Scott was a lovable rogue character and natural party starter who made everyone feel at ease and could talk to anyone, which barely concealed his alcoholic tendencies. They had been together eighteen years, married for seventeen and a half, and it had been great. Gemma had felt like the luckiest girl in the entire world; he was her best friend, her partner-in-crime, thoughtful and considerate, caring and amazing, funny, and sexy. She had always been his queen although *had* was the operative word in that sentence.

In the last fifteen months, he really turned into…what? She didn't even know herself. She went backwards and forwards often about how and what had changed in him and their relationship, but in actuality, nothing had changed about him—nothing at all. He had barely evolved, grown, or changed in the time they'd been together. He still drank daily. It did seem as though his drinking took center stage these days, and sure, she could get super pissed off and think all the horrible thoughts in the world about him, but somewhere, deep inside, she kept hoping the old Scott would come back, and their blissfully happy life would pick right back up where it left off. Where did it leave off? There wasn't really a moment in time she could pinpoint, just a gradual eroding as Scott's work responsibilities increased and his drinking picked up. He hadn't really changed so much as kind of become less— he actually seemed to stop being the full Scott she knew for so long. It was more like his joy, compassion, empathy and thoughtfulness had gradually been eroded as his drinking and recovering from his drinking took up more and more of his time, thoughts, and energy. Did that make him an alcoholic? Gemma didn't really think so. He still worked hard, paid the bills, and besides, he didn't drink all day.

*****

"If you're not careful, you'll end up totally codependent," Celia had told her one day. *That* had just pissed her off, and she cut her visit short on that day. But what if she was right? Gemma didn't really know what codependent meant, but it just sounded awful. When she had gotten home that day, she googled it and came across one of those "Six Sure Signs of a Codependent Relationship" articles. She felt relieved when she didn't identify with any of the six signs, except maybe one of them—finding it difficult to say no to a partner's demands on time and energy. But wasn't that just a part of marriage?

Chapter 2

Not-So-Happy Home

She was actually pleasantly surprised to see Scott's car in the driveway when they pulled in, although that didn't last long. Any momentary fantasies she had of him having been to the supermarket and/or cooking dinner were gone as fast as they'd popped into her head. He was passed out on the couch, beer in one hand, remote control in the other. There were no groceries in the kitchen, the cat was on the counter, and the TV was on ESPN blaring some uncomfortably loud sports show where men yelled at each other about football or basketball players or some other sport. Noah reached over and took the remote without saying anything. She was slightly disturbed on some level that their son wasn't even concerned at his dad's state.

Does he see it so often that he thinks it's normal for our family?

Gemma walked over to Scott and kissed him on the cheek, taking the beer bottle out of his hand and putting it on the coffee table,

"Honey." She shook him lightly. "Scott, wake up."

He took a deep breath in and started to open his eyes. They were bloodshot, and his breath smelt like pure alcohol. She hoped he hadn't driven home in that state. Even as she was having that thought, she knew that he had.

"Did you drive home that buzzed?"

"I'm fine." He sat up, protesting.

"Um, I disagree." Gemma shook her head. "Did you get to the supermarket? Like you said you would? Did you even buy milk? Or bread?" She could hear her tone rising, accusatory and bitchy.

Scott stood up, indignant "You know I haven't been, why do you have to start as soon as you get home?" He shot her an accusing, barely focused look. "You knew I was busy this afternoon, why didn't *you* do it?"

"Because you said you would! And I didn't think *brunch* took all afternoon!" Gemma could hear herself loud and indignant and suddenly felt impatient, angry, ignored, and let down all at the same time. "Dammit, Scott! It's dinner time, and it's Sunday! We have no food for lunches, and I still have to put the laundry in the dryer and—"

"Why are you always so negative? Bitch, bitch, bitch like I don't do anything around here! I make all the money! What the hell is your problem?"

"What the hell is my problem? What the hell is *your* problem? What makes you so damn special and exempt from everything around here?" She repeated the question, feeling attacked and defensive, she went on, "You really want to know what my problem is? My problem is that you can't keep your word anymore! My problem is that you act like this is a freaking hotel! And you think you don't have to do anything around here but show up! Who do you think you are?"

Noah turned the TV up to drown out the fighting and put his hands over his ears. Gemma felt guilty; he hated it when they argued.

"Turn it down, Noah!" Scott yelled at him, as he reached over to snatch the remote out of the little boys hand. He missed though, lurched forward, and stood up a little fast and a little unsteady. Noah flinched like he'd been hit. Gemma shot Scott an accusing look. He continued, "I didn't promise you anything. You knew I was meeting friends, why do you always do this? It's not my fault I have a life and you don't!" He spat out the last sentence and stormed out of the room, slamming the door.

Ouch. Gemma flinched internally. That one hurt.

*****

Since they had moved, Gemma had a hard time making any meaningful friendships—except Celia, if having a friend you only got to see/talk to every couple of months counted for anything. By fluke, they had met when Gemma was called in last minute to work on a wedding when they first moved here. Celia was the bubbly hairdresser cracking jokes with a cheeky grin and something good to say about everyone. They had instantly hit it off. Celia's car wouldn't start after they finished the job, and Gemma had given her a ride home. It was an instant friendship which Gemma presumed would be indicative of her life in the South. So far, that thought had been incorrect.

Making friends was something she had never had a problem with previously in life. Somehow she had arrived at a place where between working full time and being the main caregiver to Noah, as well as family accountant, taxi driver, concierge, housekeeper, and cook, she never had any time to go out and "make" new friends. Scott had always been her social circle/best friend/lover. She'd never needed anyone else—until now, obviously.

In the months since they had relocated for Scott's job, he'd been more and more involved with his work friends and social time and less and less involved with Gemma and Noah.

At first, Gemma was understanding. Yes, it was tough for him to step into the GM role at Marshside Mama's, a hugely popular restaurant that had three other branches up and down the eastern seaboard but was brand-new to this town and took a lot of his time and energy, but as his promises of "family time" and "I'll make it up to you, babe" stretched out over weeks and then months, Gemma felt ignored and resentful—discarded and forgotten. She had tried everything she could think of—counseling (that lasted only a few months as Scott had let slip that he was only doing it for her as "he was fine, it was Gemma that had the problem"), regular date nights (which had gone from once every two weeks to monthly and less, even then his phone came too, and he was on it all night, which made Gemma feel even more invisible to him). She had tried planning romantic nights in, cooking his favorite dinners, offering time and ideas of all the things they used to like to do together—ten-pin bowling, riding their bikes, beach days, hiking, day trips—but there was always something more important demanding his time.

As time passed and she kept turning to Scott for conversation, friendship, comfort, support, and general input into family life, he resisted and argued and stayed out drinking. It occurred to her that Scott's problem was not workaholic in nature, it was alcoholic.

He had always enjoyed a drink. His family were drinkers, all of them, so it was completely normal to him. It was something Gemma and Scott had spoken about often over the course of their time together. It was how he made his living when they first met. Scott was a bartender and a very good one for the first ten years of their relationship. He was funny, personable, good under pressure, could make anyone feel comfortable, share a joke or talk about the topics of the day. He was magnetic, sexy, and a generally great guy. He also had a great work ethic and quickly worked his way up the ladder at Marshside Mama's, he accepted his first promotion when Gemma was pregnant with Noah.

"I can't sling drinks forever, right, babe? I want to step up and provide a good life for our little family." Gemma was hugely proud of him and supported him all along the way, from bar manager to duty manager to assistant restaurant manager to manager. The owners knew he was a sure thing and groomed him well over the nine years he had worked for them—until finally they came to him with "an offer he couldn't refuse" to relocate to Coastal Carolina in a bold move by Marshside Mama's. He was promoted to general manager opening a brand-new location in the South, it could not fail. And it didn't; business was booming.

Scott had been so excited when he shared the offer with her eighteen months ago that he had bought her favorite champagne and roses to break the news of the promotion, and she was excited too. Noah was six at the time so it seemed as good a time as any to move. Their relocating costs were covered, and they even were given a house to live in (well, rent at a reduced rate). Gemma was a makeup artist for a popular line at a department store so she had no problem finding work once they arrived. At first it was wonderful, idyllic even. Gemma and Scott and Noah were happy and settling in to their new locale and life—until little by little, things started to go a bit...sideways.

Scott was always at work or drinking or both. He had little to no interest in Gemma or Noah or their lives. At first, he would offer genuine concern and excuses—"had to show up as GM," "had to boost staff morale," "had to work to build the team"—then he would call at the last minute with work issues that needed his attention and miss out on events with Noah such as baseball games and cub scouts. Gemma hated seeing him so disappointed in his dad, so she would try and make excuses for Scott until one day it occurred to her that she was teaching Noah that she was firmly in denial about Scott's choices and drinking. So she stopped lying to Noah. Above all else, she did not want her son thinking it was normal, acceptable even, for a wife to lie about her husband's choices and decisions.

She knew he knew and observed far more than she cared to admit.

Gemma didn't talk badly about Scott's choices to Noah, she just stopped making excuses for his lack of presence in their family life.

*****

Scott didn't appreciate Gemma's new honest approach with their son. He grew up in a "traditional" 1980s middle-class home—Mom worked part-time and was the primary caregiver of Scott and his siblings, Dad was a busy dentist in a small town. His father worked hard and long hours but also had license to "blow off steam" when he felt it necessary. His wife knew her duty as mother and woman of the house, just like her mother and his mother before them. She never questioned her husband's choices. He was the "man of the house," the main breadwinner. Scott's mother was never consulted on big decisions or even any decisions to do with the family nor did she ever question that fact, she simply "knew her place." It was part of the reason why Scott had found Gemma so attractive when they first met, aside from the fact that she was stunningly beautiful with her deep hazel eyes that seemed to look straight into his soul and long, rich chestnut hair. She knew herself and knew what she wanted. She was strong and bold, funny and intelligent. Scott had never met anyone like her before. She was everything his mother and all the women in his family and previous girlfriends were not. She was a challenge, and she challenged him continually to be a better person. He fell in love with her almost immediately—not that he would ever admit that to anyone.

He had loved her more than anyone or anything he'd ever loved before. She was his perfect mirror, or so he had thought, for over a decade. It wasn't until Noah started growing up, then she changed—became more demanding and full of criticism, always banging on about this, that, or the other, asking him questions, wanting to know his every move. "Scott, why don't you do this? Why are you doing that? Where did you go after work? What were you thinking?" He felt she didn't respect him at all. He was doing really well at work, everyone respected him there. Why did *she* always talk down to him and expect him to give up his free time to do boring stuff around the house or with her? They'd spent plenty of time together in the past, what was her problem now? He worked long hours and deserved some time off with his friends and coworkers. They knew him, they respected him. He'd stayed the same. It was Gemma that had changed. He just didn't get why she was so darn needy all the time.

He didn't want to come home and solve problems, he got paid to do that at work!

It wasn't like what she did was that hard. His was the demanding job, *he* deserved the time off with friends. He only drank to relax and unwind. He wasn't an alcoholic or anything. All throughout his bar career, he had known people with way bigger problems with alcohol than his drinking. He was fine, he was totally in control. He just didn't understand why she had such a problem with him wanting to have some downtime with his friends. Why did she have to control everything in his life all the time?

*****

Gemma stared down the hall at the closed bedroom door, wondering if she should just storm down there and tell him how unreasonable he was being! Who the hell did he think he was? Treating her like this?

"Mom, I'm hungry," Noah announced, snapping Gemma out of her head. She closed the door to the hallway and let out a sigh suddenly feeling defeated. Noah came over and wrapped his arms around her waist. "I love you, Mom. Can you stop fighting now?" He looked up at her with his big chocolate brown eyes. She leaned down and kissed him on the head.

"I love you too." Suddenly feeling guilty, she said, "I'm sorry, Noah, I hate fighting too. I promise, no more fighting tonight."

Noah gave her a smile, "Can I play on your phone?" Gemma handed it to him. Noah ran and jumped onto the couch.

"Okay, son, what shall we eat?" she half-said to herself.

She looked in the cupboard, fridge, and freezer, seeing what she could cobble together for a relatively nutritious meal. "All righty, how about mac and cheese, chicken nuggets, and carrot sticks?"

"Can we just have mac and cheese?" Noah asked hopefully. Gemma shook her head, knowing full well that's probably all he was going to eat anyway.

She got busy making dinner for them,

"Scott!" She opened the door to the hall and yelled, "*Scott!* Are you hungry? Do you want some dinner?"

No answer. She wondered if he'd even eaten today.

She walked down the hall toward their bedroom door. She didn't know what to expect as she opened the door, but she wasn't surprised. Scott was passed out across the bed, snoring. Gemma kneeled down next to the bed and stroked his hair. She kissed his forehead. As she did so, he half-rolled over, trying to put his arm around her. Gemma let herself be held awkwardly for a moment.

"I love you, Scott Harris. Why are you doing this?" she whispered into his ear as she edged out from under his arm.

Gemma closed the door and went back to the kitchen.

The pot was boiling, and she continued making dinner, the hot tears running down her face. This was not how she'd imagined their night together. She thought they would cook dinner together and catch up. She had so many things to tell him and talk to him about.

Scott was barely ever home. That stupid restaurant took up all his time, she was lucky if he was here one or two nights a week. Why did he just go and get wasted all the time so they never got to see each other? Didn't he want to hang out with her? They hadn't had a decent conversation in weeks. Or sex. They used to make love at least a few times a week. Didn't he want her anymore? *How did it come to this?*

That night, she fell asleep in Noah's bed with him, book and all. He was snuggled into her arm. She woke in the middle of the night and could hear Scott still snoring from the next room. She gently closed the book, eased her arm out from under Noah, went into their room, and took off Scott's shoes. She pulled the blanket up and kissed his cheek. She sat on the edge of the bed for a while, watching him, then went back into Noah's room. Gary, their grey and white cat, watched her with his green eyes. His deep purr rumbled from his chest from his spot at the end of Noah's bed.

She climbed back into bed next to Noah and decided to just stay there, where there was no snoring. Just peaceful purring, and sweet little boy breathing. It was warm and strangely comforting lying next to her son. She kissed him on the forehead and listened to his breathing, Gary's purring, and Scott snoring in the next room as she thought about everything, trying to figure out where it had all gone wrong. How had they become so distant? Was his drinking out of control? Why didn't Scott want to help around the house anymore? Was she overreacting? Was Scott right? Was she just really negative these days? Was she wrong to expect more of him in their family life? Had they ever actually talked about their ideas and roles in their own family? Didn't he want to be a good dad? Had they ever discussed their expectations from each other once they had kids? Should they have done that? Gemma wondered why she hadn't ever seen this coming, she was very perceptive and a good judge of character, there was nothing in all their time together that had even indicated his total lack of interest in being a family guy. Why wasn't he interested in being with them anymore? Was he having an affair? Why wasn't he interested in being with her anymore? Why didn't he talk to her anymore? Why did he cut her off whenever she tried to talk to him? Was it all in her head? Was she expecting too much of him? She felt confident he was not having an affair. He was so busy with his work and his drinking that she didn't honestly see how he could fit *that* in—or want to. He had always taken pride in his appearance, but so had she. After all, they both worked in fields where personal grooming was directly beneficial to their pay packet.

She missed the old Scott, her friend and keeper of secrets. He always knew exactly what to say to put it all in perspective. He used to laugh at her overthinking everything while wrapping his arms around her and kissing her on the forehead with an "It's all right, kiddo, we got this," and she would instantly feel at ease. Just knowing they had each other meant they could face or work out anything. Maybe they just needed some alone time together, a night away somewhere. They used to go away together all the time. She was sure if they could just get together and be truly alone for a while, they would remember what it was they loved about each other. She also thought about Celia's frying pan theory. What was God using her for? What was he throwing at her to perfect? Was he tempering her marriage?

Or was it just her? Gemma had always believed she was the luckiest girl in the world, as she had found the only husband she would ever have. From the beginning, it was so easy and normal and natural. They used to have such a great time together. He used to make her laugh so hard she'd think she was going to pee her pants. She couldn't wait to grow old with him. It felt like they were still only at the beginning for at least fifteen years. Fifteen years! It's a long time to feel secure and well matched! What did it feel like now? Gemma wished there was someone she could talk to about all of this! But who? She tried to pinpoint the moment it all started going wrong. She couldn't think of anyone she wanted to bare her soul to. She wished it could be Scott! Her thoughts churned for a long time until sleep finally came.

In the morning, she woke early, stiff and sore with a dead arm, in exactly the same position as she had finally fallen asleep in. She eased her arm out from under Noah's head, planting a kiss on his cheek. He was so beautiful when he was asleep, so innocent. She could hear Gary meowing in the kitchen and Scott making coffee. She made her way quietly down the hall into the kitchen.

"Hey," she said.

"Hey, honey, I missed you in bed," he replied and carried on before she could say anything. "I went and got some coffee for us, as well bread and milk and cereal so you can make Noah's breakfast, and I can give him some money to take to school to get lunch." Scott offered a shy smile.

Gemma smiled back. "Wow, you must have gotten up early. Thanks." She didn't know what to say. It wasn't exactly everything they needed to get through the week, but it would get the day started. She appreciated the effort and thought behind it and felt grateful there was a twenty-four-hour supermarket not too far from their home. She looked down at her hands.

Scott stepped closer and hugged her. "I'm sorry, honey." She felt warm and safe in his arms. Gemma leaned into him.

"I didn't mean to get so drunk yesterday. I was tired and hadn't seen Steve for a while, and we ran into a couple that had just started at Marshside Mama's, so I stayed a little too long and drank a little too much…" He trailed off. "Forgive me?" He cupped her face as she looked at him.

Gemma looked deep into his chocolate brown eyes. She wanted to forgive him. Everyone makes mistakes, and she felt awful.

"I guess." She still felt disappointed and abandoned.

"I'll tell you what," he continued. "Wednesday, I'm only doing the lunch shift at work. Why don't you get a babysitter and we can go out early for an appetizer and a glass of wine together? We must be overdue for some sort of date night."

"Really?" Gemma asked, feeling her spirits lift. That sounded like a great idea. She hadn't had him to herself in ages. She felt herself brighten. "Okay," she said, "let's do it."

He kissed her on the forehead and wrapped his arms around her. She breathed in his scent and breathed out a big sigh.

The rest of the day went by in a happy blur. Gemma fought off any doubts and succumbed to the feeling that maybe they were back on track, and things were going to be all right.

Chapter 3

New Friends

Wednesday evening rolled around quickly, and Gemma was excited as she got ready to go out with Scott. It had been such a long time since she had gone out anywhere besides work. The babysitter arrived, and after going over the usual supper and bedtime instructions, they headed out.

Scott opened the car door for her and told her how great she looked. She felt unexpectedly nervous and was looking forward to their time together.

"Where shall we go?" she asked expectantly. Scott suggested a place he knew not far from Marshside Mama's.

They headed over to a little sushi bar about a block or so from the restaurant. It was run by a Japanese couple who were very friendly and seemed excited to meet Scott's wife. Gemma was flattered and asked Scott how they knew him so well. Apparently, he came here during the week often for lunch with one of the owners from Marshside Mama's, Rob Mckay, when he was in town to get "off-campus" and discuss work, away from work. Rob was a friendly older gentleman who had been in the restaurant business forever. The rumor was he was gay. Nobody ever saw him with a lady—or anyone for that matter. He was always perfectly dressed and groomed and very personable but very focused and goal-oriented—which had obviously worked for him, as he was now part owner of a very successful chain of restaurants. Gemma had always admired his professionalism. He managed to walk the fine line between being accessible and professional but keeping his private life private.

They sat at the sushi bar, and Scott ordered them some sake to share. They ordered their sushi and chatted pleasantly about stuff. Gemma searched for depth and meaning in their conversation. Scott seemed happy (or was it distracted?) to keep it to the superficial level. He kept looking past her, watching people come in, so much so she even turned around to see what he was looking at.

"What is it?" Scott asked, looking at her.

"Would you rather be somewhere else?" she asked, searching his face for something to give away what was going on in his head.

"Good grief, woman, do you have to overthink everything?" He gave her a quizzical look.

She laughed. "Okay, okay, maybe I am." She breathed out heavily, not realizing she had been holding her breath. "So how is work going?" Gemma asked with a pang of guilt she hadn't even made an effort to ask him how his own work was going.

"Well, babe, you know, I'm really just the head babysitter." He told her about his managers, their particular quirks and various mini-dramas involved with their positions—Mark the bar manager who had just gotten engaged to his pregnant girlfriend Katie, who wanted to get married before the baby came, Sooz, the butch, tattooed and talented head chef who dominated the all-male kitchen, and Ryan the restaurant manager and his assistant general manager. They talked about the new wait staff they had hired, including a couple called Janine, who was a waitress, and her husband Daniel, who was a bartender. He thought they were a fun couple, and that Gemma and Janine would get on.

Gemma was interested in hearing about his workmates, putting backstories to the names she heard him mention often. It had been hard for her to make any friends here. All her friends and social circles for most of the last twenty years had stemmed from their workplaces, especially Scott's. It was habit back in the day, before Noah, for her to go to his workplace after she finished at hers and get something to eat or have a glass of wine and wait for him to finish. Even after Noah was born, he was always so proud to have her and Noah drop by and see him at work. He always made her feel welcome, introduced them to everyone, and she knew she was an important part of his life. Again, *had* was the operative word. Now she didn't know anyone he worked with or anyone that worked for him. She'd heard names but had no clue what these people looked like or were like. Initially, she had put it down to Scott being so busy with the new restaurant and all the responsibilities that went with it.

Their meal arrived, and they ate. Scott ordered more sake, and Gemma ordered water, mindful of the time. She tried to talk about Noah and home life, but Gemma was aware Scott was just being polite. He kind of blew her off with an "I know you can handle it, babe. You're a natural." All in all, though, it was a pleasant evening with her husband, and yes, maybe she was overthinking everything.

She felt somewhat miffed, however, at his continual disinterest in his family's life, but again, she put it down to him being so busy and consumed with all things Marshside Mama's. It was a huge operation and was getting busier and busier—business was booming.

They paid their tab, and Gemma excused herself to use the restroom. When she came out Scott was standing at the bar talking to a couple, Gemma sidled up beside him, putting her arm around his waist. As he introduced her to them, the woman handed him a beer. What do you know, it was Janine and Daniel in the flesh. Gemma said, "Hello," and observed them both. They were engrossed in their "work" conversation. The bartender lined up three shot glasses and reached for the liquor bottles behind him. *Huh, they didn't waste any time there, she thought, I wasn't gone that long!*

Janine was a flirty blond with blue eyes and a very tight shirt. The buttons straining to keep her shirt closed over her ample chest. She was taller than Daniel, her husband. He had black hair and a black manicured goatee beard. His shirt was also pretty tight. She could tell the two of them were legends in their own lunchtimes.

Gemma made small talk with them, but they were all mainly talking about work situations and people. Gemma was clueless. She struggled to feel relevant in the conversation. They all did a shot together. Scott caught her frown as he put down his glass. She gave him a "Where's mine?" look. He laughed and put his arm around her. "Sorry, babe."

"Let's have another one!" Janine raised her glass, and Daniel picked his up, both of them looking to Scott, who nodded to the bartender. "And one for the little woman," he said, motioning to Gemma. She started to protest but figured one wouldn't hurt. She did a quick mental calculation of how much she'd had to drink in the timeframe they'd been there. It was still only eight fifteen, and they had planned on being home by nine, so they had time.

They all did a big "cheers," and she threw back the tequila as she used to many years before. She figured she was at least ten to twelve years older than the both of them. She knew she held her age well. Being a makeup artist and skincare consultant gave her valuable knowledge (and products). Still, age was harsh on women, there was no doubting that, and she really wasn't interested in drinking and partying as they had more than ten years ago. She'd much rather hang out at home with close friends, a couple of glasses of wine, and some intelligent conversation. She had done her "bar" time, partied her butt off with the best of them, and had some crazy stories to tell. It had been a blast, but she was not looking to recreate those days. Gemma was more interested in this chapter in life and raising a family. She wondered if Scott still was too.

Gemma pulled up a bar stool next to Scott but felt a little left out when he kept angling away from her. She put her hand on the small of his back, and he stepped back a little. She figured she may as well get comfortable and tried to follow along with the people and stories they were talking about from Marshside Mama's. She tried to keep up but seriously wasn't that interested. Good grief, it sounded like they were talking about high school!

And much like when she was in high school, she feigned interest to keep up with the "in" crowd but was bored out of her mind. She kept glancing sideways at Scott, not quite believing that he was just as gossipy as they were!

This wasn't "her" Scott! He had never really cared about being one of the "cool kids" before! They used to poke fun at the people he worked with that bought into all of that superficial crap. Yet here she was, watching him carry on like the other two! He ordered another beer.

"Honey, we gotta go in about twenty minutes."

He winked at her. "Don't panic, babe, that's plenty of time to finish this."

Gemma stuck to her water and turned toward the three with a vaguely interested smile on her face, not wanting to appear too judgmental or standoffish or desperate. She joined the conversation where she could, asking questions here and there. They all obviously knew each other better than she knew them. She found the usual trick of asking someone continually about themselves was the best way to have Janine talk to her. Janine and Daniel had been married for four years and together for six. They had two kids, a boy (Thomas) and a girl (Zoe) aged six and four. (Gemma tried to do the quick math on those pregnancies but let it go.) Originally from California, Janine had moved east to go to university and came here after graduation. Working in hospitality was far more lucrative than her bachelor's degree ever would be, Gemma understood that one. She often had gone back to the restaurant/bar business herself for a summer to make some quick cash. Daniel was from North Carolina. They had met at the beach and ended up being neighbors and working together that summer. Daniel obviously adored her. She wondered briefly what Janine saw in him—besides his incredible grooming. She laughed to herself, at how judge-y she was being. *Wow, that superficial crap is contagious*, she thought with a silent chuckle.

Janine obviously enjoyed being the center of attention. She wasn't exactly a "girl's" girl. Gemma estimated she was in her early thirties. Any attempts Gemma made to have a deeper conversation with her, about anything other than Janine, she seemed to not hear her, too busy talking to all the guys—even the bartender—about herself. And deliberately brown nosing the boss! Laughing so fake and loud at Scott's jokes, even when they weren't funny! Despite this obvious character flaw, Gemma thought she seemed nice enough. Maybe they could be friends. Maybe. Janine's behavior made Gemma feel a little left out. She was over it and wanted to go home. Scott seemed to be having a great time—was that his third or fourth shot? He was completely oblivious to Gemma's discomfort. He didn't even look at her. He was definitely in his work zone—charming, funny and the life of the party.

She finished her water, put down her glass, and checked her watch. 8:55 p.m.

"All right, babe." She cleared her throat. "Time to go." Scott barely looked at her. Did he hear her? He picked up his beer and glanced at her, raising his eyebrows. Well at least it was acknowledgment. Janine and Daniel ignored her. Gemma asked for the tab, and Daniel waved her away. "Don't worry about it, we'll get it."

Scott still got out $50 and put it on the bar. Gemma knew he was a big tipper from way back. They both were—when you've worked for tips, you make sure you're generous.

He swished back the last of his beer. "All right then," he said as he picked up his cigarettes, and started saying his goodbyes.

Janine stepped in front of them, rather presumptuously. Was she doing the boob thrust thing at Scott? "Won't you just have one more for the road?"

Scott looked at Gemma, slightly hopeful. "Nope, our sitter is expecting us." She smiled at him, pointing at her watch. "We told her we'd be back by 9:00 p.m. at the latest, remember? We've got about five minutes."

Scott laughed. "Okay, hon, you got me." They said their goodbyes and headed out.

Gemma thought it best that she drove. Scott agreed.

They got home, paid the sitter, and Gemma went in to kiss Noah. He was awake and very chatty. She was a little disappointed. She had been hoping he would be asleep so that she could hang out with Scott. Of course, he needed three cuddles and for her to check the wardrobe and under the bed for monsters. She sat and stroked his head while he told her about what he did with the babysitter. She had taught him how to play a new card game. Gemma smiled to herself. *He never wants to talk to me when he gets home from school, and at bedtime, it all comes out.* She did know, however, that Noah would also fall asleep midsentence, which he did, looking so cute and tiny in his bed.

By the time Noah was asleep, Gemma estimated about twenty-five minutes had passed. She made her way into the living room. Scott was on his second beer. The whiskey bottle on the counter told her he'd had a few more shots, and he was engrossed in his phone.

"Whatcha doing?" Gemma sat next to him.

"Waiting for you. Why don't you sit down for a second? You never want to sit with me anymore." His words were running together a little slurred, his eyes somewhat glazed. He put his arm around her and drew her in for a kiss. His soft warm lips were familiar and comforting, pressing urgently onto her own. She turned her body toward him as he moved his arm to her upper back, pulling her tightly into him. Gemma responded by pressing herself into him. He put his other hand on her waist. She could feel her anticipation rising. She couldn't even remember the last time they'd had sex. Besides everything over the years, they had always had great sex.

"Let's go to bed, babe. Take me to bed," she purred.

Scott drew her in for another kiss, cradling her face. "You go wash your face and warm up the bed. I'll be right behind you," he promised.

Gemma grumbled a little, kissed him deeply and passionately again. As she got up, he patted her on the butt. "Don't take too long." She headed to the bedroom, wondering how drunk he was. She got ready for bed as fast as she could and found her last sexy negligee, laughing silently to herself, remembering when she used to wear them to bed regularly. She got herself ready, feeling excited, and climbed in bed.

"Scott," she called. No answer. "Honey, I'm ready." Nothing. Gemma got out of bed, feeling suddenly frustrated. "Scott!" She walked back down the hall into the living room. Scott was passed out on the couch. She shook him, feeling angry and disappointed. "Scott!"

He semi-stirred. "I'll be just a minute." He slurred his words together, barely opening his eyes.

"Oh my god, are you serious?" Gemma was suddenly super pissed.

"It's all right, honey, I'll be right there." Scott hardly raised his head as his words ran together. He made a half-assed attempt at pulling her close to him.

"*Scott!*" Gemma flung his arm off her and stomped off to the bedroom, slamming the door. She didn't care if she woke Noah up. How could Scott do this to her?

What the hell? She thought back to when this would *never* have happened. Scott was always ready to go, eager for any opportunity to be intimate that presented itself. She fiercely tore back the covers and got in bed. Dammit!

This was *not* the way this was supposed to have gone!

She lay in bed, angrily flipping through the channels on TV. There was nothing that interested her, she was so pissed off and frustrated and disappointed. She turned off the TV and got out of bed. Scott really had a problem! This was ridiculous! Some date night!

After walking back down the hallway into the living room, she stood for a moment, watching him sleep. What the hell was she going to do now? She sat down on the couch for a moment and shook him. "Scott?" Nothing. "Scott?" she said in a whisper, almost hoping he would wake up and come to bed. After a few minutes, she realized the futility and went to bed alone.

She lay awake for a long time, thinking about how to talk to him about this. His drinking was out of control! She reflected on the other times she had talked to him about his drinking. It had made a difference for a little while, he would make an effort to keep it under control. Would it make a difference now?

Chapter 4

Learning to Pray

Scott didn't say much about that night—a muttered apology that he felt bad and he would "make it up to her." The next morning, he was in a hurry to get to work to deal with an errant fire alarm. Noah had baseball that afternoon, and Scott was already back at work by the time they had finished and got home. Gemma couldn't find the right time or the right words to talk about his drinking, beyond a concerned parental "We really need to do something about your drinking, Scott," which sucked. She wasn't his mother! And did not want to be!

He just nodded, muttering something about how he would sit down with her and talk about it but how busy he was at work this week and blah blah blah. A few days passed and then a week, two weeks, then a month. Gemma felt frustrated at herself that she could never seem to find the right time to talk about anything. The restaurant was getting busier and busier, and her own work schedule clashed with Scott's. Unfortunately, having no family close by meant they had to work opposite schedules to be sure one of them was always available for Noah. Things kept on rolling along, which somehow translated to her being the main caregiver of everything, which was fine when she had an actual husband who was involved and present and supportive and cooperative, and she felt like she was part of a team. But now, she felt put upon, devalued, invalidated, and like it was just expected. *How did Scott suddenly turn so entitled? Seriously, what was his deal?*

Gemma went back and forth, feeling resentful and ignored. Why did she have to do all the work? Did Scott think Noah just raised himself? Fed himself, bought his own food, got himself to and from school or practice? Baseball alone was like a job, with two practices and two games a week.

Gemma struggled to keep everything together. Some days it felt so futile. She felt so invisible, like someone drowning only a few feet from the shore, watching people go about their daily lives, completely oblivious to the fact that someone was in trouble, they would see, if they would just care to look. But she knew she had to keep going—for Noah.

*****

When Scott was home, he was completely shattered from working such long hours or drinking so much, or both, or consumed by his phone. There was never a good time to talk about anything.

Gemma started to talk to God. Maybe it was praying? She would ask for strength and courage to get through each day. She had trouble sleeping and would lie awake, waiting for Scott to get home. She missed him so much. She missed his company, his friendship, his sense of humor, even just his warmth next to her at night. The restaurant kept him there later and later each night. When she'd call him, he'd tell her he was just finishing up but still wouldn't get home for an hour or so, reeking of alcohol and cigarettes. When he did climb into bed, he smelt like a bar and would snore so loudly, it would keep her awake and it was so frustrating! He wouldn't even brush his teeth or wash his hands before bed. Gemma would only end up getting three or four hours of broken sleep a night and was feeling vulnerable and emotional. Why wouldn't he just take a shower when he came home (like he used to?) or brush his teeth and wash his damn hands?

When she'd bring to up with Scott, he'd say he'd make a better effort, but he never did. Some nights he'd pass out with his stupid shoes still on, right on the couch. Gemma would always wake him up before Noah woke up. She didn't want their son to think that passing out drunk, fully clothed on the couch was a normal thing to do. Gemma was so disappointed, she didn't know which way to turn. Who do you talk to when your bestie doesn't want to be your bestie anymore?

She also felt lonely and desperate. She wasn't sure she really knew what desperate actually felt like, or was it frantic? Why was he acting like this? Did he not want to be with her and Noah? What about all they had done, and planned, and been through together? Did that mean nothing? Was she wrong in thinking they had built a great foundation to their lives so far in their relationship? Was it her fault? She cried a lot, alone in the middle of the night. And she felt pissed off, especially the nights he said he was on his way and didn't show up for over an hour.

She asked him outright one morning if he was having an affair. He laughed. "Where would I get the time?" Gemma thought he had a point, but still, she couldn't help but wonder. Especially when she knew it was merely a ten-minute drive from Marshside Mama's to their house.

When she'd talk to him about anything to do with their home or money or lives, he'd get angry and tell her she was so negative and ask why she couldn't just "handle it." After all, "he made all the money." She was really beginning to resent *that* sentence coming out of his mouth. He used it as a legitimate end to any conversation. Gemma found herself arguing almost every day with Scott. They just couldn't seem to find any common ground. She felt awful and impatient most of the time, jealous that he was so involved with everything and everyone to do with his work. Gemma prayed more and more, trying to find comfort somewhere.

The women she worked with were friendly enough, but seeing as they worked in department store retail, the only time she really got to hang out with any of them was if they had the same shifts. Otherwise, they worked opposite shifts. At Noah's afterschool activities, Gemma made an effort to make friends with the other moms. There were a couple she got on really well with, but they all worked full time and had other kids too. It was very hard to find any time to do anything with any of them. She even thought about trying to find a church. Not one like she was raised in. But she found herself remembering the sense of community. Even though it had been so dysfunctional (to her), it was still a community.

Pamela, one of the older ladies she worked with had mentioned the non-denominational church she went to that wasn't very far from where they lived. It was held in a dance studio on Sundays. They had a band and a great kid's ministry. Gemma wasn't sure what to make of that. Was that even church? Gemma realized she needed to get over the way she was taught about God, and church, and be open to the fact that there were many different ways to worship.

Still, she couldn't quite bring herself to go—just yet, anyway.

Being inherently introverted, just the thought of walking in the door terrified her. The church and worship thing was definitely on a slow simmer in her mind. She felt comfortable with leaving the fry pan set on low for now.

She was aware of needing something though. The frying pan analogy Celia had spoken of came to mind often as she observed her life, both forwards and backward. It was easy in retrospect to see when she had burned something when it was supposed to be simmering or even had it set too low in her actions when a rapid boil was needed, but right now in the present, at this point in her life, she couldn't figure out if she was burning something or didn't have the heat on at all. Or maybe it was the wrong element? Was something cooking? Or too cooked?

However, the truth remained that as Noah grew, she wanted him to have an awareness of a higher power, that there was an all-loving, all-knowing power that would always be with him and around him. She wanted him to have some sort of relationship with God as it were. Just thinking of it like that made her cringe a little—thanks to all the cliched born-again Christians that bombarded her in college—but you can't question something if you have no prior knowledge of it, right? She would talk to him about God, being the Almighty Creator, who created everything out of Love for us. She talked to him about Jesus too. Noah thought Jesus sounded pretty cool, like an ancient superhero. She asked him if he would like to go and check out a church one day to learn more about Jesus. Noah thought that would be good.

One morning in the kitchen, when the radio station would not stay on the station, she was turning the dial ever so slowly to get a clear signal. Suddenly, crystal clear, she heard a song she had never heard before. "You know the situation can't be right/And all you ever do is fight/But there's a reason that the road is long/It takes some time to make your courage strong/Hold on tight a little longer/What won't kill ya, makes ya stronger/Get back up cause it's a hard love." Gemma stood there stunned. It was a song called "Hard Love" by Needtobreathe. Wow. Could anything be more perfect? *Keep going, Gemma, you've got this.* From that morning, she became a fan of Positive Hits Christian Radio.

Noah liked the songs too. Gemma felt so much better having him listen to that in the car than the other crap that permeated the airwaves and found herself silently rejoicing when she heard him singing along in the backseat.

Maybe she would go check out that church soon.

She found herself talking to God more and more. Was it praying? She didn't think so. It didn't feel like praying. She wasn't on her knees, doing the sign of the cross as she was taught. So was she actually praying? She didn't know. Half the time it was as she was driving or lying awake in the middle of the night. The demons of doubt and fear always came at 3 a.m. The only way she could vanquish them always started with "I don't know if you're listening God."

It just felt right to talk to God. She didn't know if he was listening. Had she ever known? All she knew was it felt good to feel like someone was there, even if she was just pretending. Or is that what God's love was supposed to feel like? It occurred to her she had never really been taught what God's love was supposed to feel like. She was just supposed to behave like she knew it was always there, but was it?

Chapter 5

God and Love

When they went to Celia's house next, the days were a little cooler. The balcony at the back of her house looked like nature had decorated perfectly for fall with red and orange leaves dangling from the trees. There was so much more of her neighbor's backyards and houses visible now, all five kids were playing under the balcony running in and out of the garage and up the hill in the back.

They were full of energy and laughter, plotting and joking all on the same side. It was nice to hear.

Celia had been working on collecting leaves earlier in the day with the kids for craft projects, and they were in a shoe box on the table—brilliant golds, yellows, orange and reds looked like a box of jewels. There were also painted mini gourds sitting on the railing. The funny expressions on their faces made it look like they were witnessing something amazing—or crazy.

Celia and Gemma were drinking herbal tea and discussing life, the universe, and God as usual.

Gemma was happy once again for the break from the rest of her life. She was still thinking about going to the community church Pamela had told her about. She talked to God (prayed?) constantly. She had stopped questioning what it was, it just felt right.

"Where do you think God is?" Gemma asked Celia with a questioning glance. "Like, do you think he's in the universe or in us? Do you think he's, you know, floating above us? Or on a cloud somewhere, just watching us all—okay, well, *that* sounds very childlike."

Gemma caught herself and thought back to how she remembered thinking of God as a child, Him floating on a big cloud watching everyone and everything all the time, with bolts of lightning ready to throw them down like spears to get the sinners and baddies. She had never really questioned that interpretation of him as she grew up, it just sort of evolved, but she had never consciously questioned it, until then.

As she matured, however, and paid attention to the moment and the majesty of nature, whether it was hiking in the woods, snowboarding on a bluebird powder day, sitting at the beach, watching a sunrise or sunset, or even just taking a moment throughout the day to watch the clouds, she felt closer to God and more like she was in a church than she ever remembered feeling in a building. These moments felt better to her than being in church had. She definitely felt closer to God in nature. She felt His presence all around her but still didn't know how to explain it. She just felt it and knew.

Celia stayed silent, giving her friend space to follow her thoughts.

Gemma thought for a moment longer, trying to define where exactly she thought God dwelled. "Do you think he's in us?"

Celia nodded and started slowly. "You know, I think he is. But not in a weirdo we-are-god kind of way, but more of a God-consciousness way. To put it very simply, I think that the ego is the devil and appeals to us in a selfish, 'me, me, me' mindset, whereas if we are still and humble and really tune into others, that opens us to the God consciousness that is in all of us, which is love. When we tune into love and act with love and treat each other with love, then we are in our God consciousness. I think it's called many different things—light, universe, source energy, higher power—but really it's all *love,* and it's there for *all* of us. It's in all of us. It's all around us all the time."

Gemma liked that idea. "But what about love for your husband or partner? Does it conflict with that?"

Celia shook her head. "No, of course not, this is universal love for humanity and the earth and all of creation. Nothing ever comes into being without love." She continued, explaining her idea further, "Someone has a love for something, whether it's an interest, desire, or need. It all stems from love—a love for making things better or, seeing them evolve, or come into existence." She glanced at Gemma. "Any creative process for good or evil can be likened to the whole process of conception, gestation, and giving birth. Think about it, everything—plants, trees, people, animals, inventions, productions, buildings, scientific discoveries, medical advancements, wars, everything! And whether it's a love for humanity and the bigger picture or a selfish misdirected love, it all starts with love." Celia thought for a moment.

Gemma wasn't sure what she thought of that one. On some level, she felt resistant to this idea. Celia went on sensing Gemma's hesitancy. "Think about it. How does anything ever come into being or come to fruition?" Celia asked her.

Gemma thought about it. "Someone has an idea."

"And?" Celia prompted. "Where does the idea come from?"

"Something they're interested in? A need? A want?" Gemma offered.

Celia nodded. "I believe it stems from a basic desire to change, invent, or make easier for everyone or just themselves, to make things better. And why would you want to make things better or help someone or a bunch of people?"

Gemma understood. "Because they care."

Celia smiled. "Yes, and why do you care about anything or anyone?" She raised her eyebrows at Gemma.

"Love?" she offered halfheartedly. She couldn't understand how love, well, love the way she thought of it—man, woman, sex, partners-for-life type love—could really bring anything besides children into world.

"You do realize there are so many more kinds of love than family and marriage love, right?" Gemma was surprised by Celia's insight. Was she that transparent?

"I've never really thought about it,' she admitted.

"Well, think!" Celia challenged. She went on, repeating herself to define her thoughts.

"Someone is interested in something and devotes more and more time to learning about it and understanding it because they love it. It stimulates them, keeps them up at night, wakes them early. They lose all track of time working on it, and from that point, they have such insight that they realize it can be made better or actually invented to fill a need, so they invent it. You could, say, give birth to a project or design or thing or concept, but it all stems from love. Think about the people you know of who absolutely love what they do or teach, like the teachers in high school that loved their particular subject. They loved it so much and were so enthused about wanting to share it that it drew you in, and you found or find yourself totally interested even if it's something that didn't interest you previously. It's their *love* for their passion that gives it life and makes it interesting to the onlooker, don't you think?" Celia picked up her mug, and took a sip, watching Gemma process what she just said.

"You know," Gemma ventured, "you have a point. I have just never thought of it that way before. Everything around us was brought into existence by love...wow." Gemma's thoughts flashed to all the film and television work she had previously done and how exciting it was to work with directors and film crews who had clear direction and passion for what they were doing. Celia had a valid point.

"Pretty deep, huh?" Celia winked at her with a smirk. Gemma rolled her eyes.

She too took a sip from her cup, and continued scanning her memories, thinking about various teachers and lecturers she'd had in school and university who were so passionate about their subject, you couldn't help but be interested too. That one person's passion for a thing was attractive and then made it attractive to others. Maybe that's why Scott was so attractive. Was it his passion for creating other people's good times? *Yeah*, she cut herself off, *as long as it involves alcohol.*

On the way home, Gemma kept thinking about love and attraction, in general trying to apply the idea to all of her life. What was she passionate about? She used to love doing makeup, working on set, film shoots, etc. It was always so exciting, feeling like part of a team, a cog in the wheel helping the production machine keep turning, producing great (and sometimes not so great) things, changing the way people saw themselves, helping them transform into their characters, feeling part of something. She had definitely loved doing that. It was effortless and filled her with energy, even at the end of a long day on set, she would still feel energized and invigorated. Then there was her relationship with Scott. She had always felt like part of something bigger with him—their plans and adventures, their lives together in general. But that seemed like a lifetime ago. Now she was a cosmetic salesperson, a show pony for the department store and line she represented, selling to and educating disgruntled old women and timid yet curious teenagers, making her best effort to meet the daily numbers as required by the line she worked for. What else? What gave her life meaning? Could she even remember? Her family? Her home? Her job? She looked at Noah in the rearview mirror. Definitely her son.

She didn't even know what she liked to do for fun. What did she love? What inspired her?

This made her head spin. She felt lost and couldn't even start to fathom how she had become joyless and uninspired.

Chapter 6

Getting Social

As she pulled into the driveway, she was surprised to see Scott's car, as well as another vehicle she didn't recognize. She figured it out almost instantly as she could see Scott talking to Janine at the front door. Noah was curious but excited.

"Who's here? Dad's home!" He sprang out of the car and ran up the stairs to the front door. Gemma barely stopped the car.

"Noah! Don't leap out of the car while it's still moving!"

"Sorry, Mom!" He barely slowed his pace. Gemma watched him bound up the stairs two at a time. He sure loved his dad.

Scott reached for Noah and mussed up his hair. "How are you doing, sport?" He introduced Janine to Noah, who stuck out his hand with a polite "Nice to meet you" as Gemma walked up the stairs.

"Hello! I've heard all about you." Janine smiled, shaking Noah's hand. "Hi, Gemma," Janine said.

"Hi." Gemma smiled back. She did not know what to make of this unexpected visit. As an introvert, Gemma hated unexpected visitors. As Janine turned to walk down the stairs, she gave Scott a "what is she doing here?" look. Janine was wearing workout clothes—tight leggings with cutouts on the sides and a tight tank top, that barely covered her ample, ridiculously perky breasts. They *have totally got to be fake*, Gemma thought to herself.

"Guess what? We're pretty much neighbors now!" Janine bounced down the stairs.

"Huh?" Gemma didn't understand.

"We just moved into the house on the corner!" Janine flashed Gemma a big smile. "I just stopped by to invite you guys over for a cookout tonight. Noah can meet Thomas and Zoe, we can hang out, it'll be great! I've got wine!"

Gemma looked at her watch and then at Scott. "I don't know, Noah's got school tomorrow. It's already nearly 5:00 p.m." She felt put on the spot, all eyes expectantly on her.

Scott shrugged his shoulders. "It's just across the road, we can walk, you can bring him home after he eats."

"Please, Mom?" Noah begged, jumping up and down excited.

"Yeah, come on, Gemma. Daniel has the grill on now." Janine batted her eyelashes at her (*wow, did she really just do that?*). Gemma didn't like the way she was suddenly put in the position to be the killjoy and wreck everyone's good time.

"Well, I guess a couple of hours won't hurt," she agreed reluctantly.

"Awesome, we'll see you soon!" Janine hopped into her car and reversed down the driveway, stereo blaring.

Gemma turned to Scott and Noah, who were already heading back inside. Gemma didn't know what had just happened, she felt railroaded.

"So what was that about?" Gemma asked.

"What was what about?" Scott asked innocently. The TV was on football, and he had a beer on the coffee table.

"How did she know where we lived?" Gemma was curious, was he telling people where their house was? They had always valued their privacy, always happy to be out and about but more happy to retreat to their own sanctuary of home. Scott never told the people he managed where he lived before, and Gemma was grateful for the separation of his work and their family life.

"I don't know, saw the car I guess. I may have mentioned the neighborhood we lived in when Janine mentioned they were moving.," he offered.

That made no sense to Gemma. *How did where Janine and her family were moving to and where we live ever "just come up" in a work situation? How did Janine know Scott's car? Why is Scott letting down his guard like that? Does he talk about me at work?* She was lost obsessing in her own thoughts. Again.

"It's just a cookout with our new neighbors, it's not a test or anything." Scott walked past her, patting her on the butt. He went to the fridge and started loading a couple of beers into a bag. "Don't look so concerned," he joked.

She shook off her doubts, making an effort to see this as a good thing and not be suspicious. What was there to be suspicious of anyway? A friendly neighbor?

"What do we need to take?" Gemma asked.

Scott replied, "It's all good, Janine said they had enough food for all of us. They even have beer and wine.

"Okay." Gemma sighed. Maybe this won't be so bad. She quashed any doubts and admitted she was kind of excited and curious to be invited somewhere as a family.

Maybe she would make a friend in the neighborhood!

And she was interested to meet all his employees, see what they were like as people. Put faces to names.

"All righty, let's go." They all walked out the door together, Noah running excitedly in front.

When they got to Janine and Daniel's house, Janine met them at the door with a big "Come in! Make yourself at home!" She told Scott that Daniel, Ryan, Nick, Trent and Tom were outside, waving him through the living room toward the open sliding glass doors.

Janine looked at Noah. "Do you like Minecraft?"

Noah nodded vigorously.

"Well, you're going to love Thomas's room!' she enthused. "Let's find my kids and you can meet them."

Noah followed her through the living room to the hallway toward…the bedrooms? They didn't have to go far; a flurry of children came charging down the hall.

"Whoa, Mister!" Janine said, grabbing the first child.

Gemma was unsure what she should do. She could see the outside area where the men were, she didn't feel she'd be welcome out there. From where she was still standing in the entryway, she could see to the other side of the living area was the kitchen, the house was similar in layout to her own, so she walked around the corner, suddenly feeling really out of place and not sure what to do with herself.

Gemma was surprised at how many people were there. She could see three other kids running around, two younger and blond (Gemma presumed they were Thomas and Zoe) and another little girl in a pretty floral dress. Janine came back and haphazardly introduced her to everyone, whether they were paying attention or not. The girl in the pretty dress was Kelly's little girl, Erin, who was a year younger than Noah. Kelly was also a waitress at Marshside Mama's. She was probably about twenty-nine or thirty with bright red hair (dyed) and a cute face. She also was very tattooed, all of one arm and shoulder and back of her neck elaborately decorated with beautiful flowers and various other designs. There was also Jacob, who was a bartender, and Ashley his girlfriend who worked behind the bar as well. They were both also in their late twenties or early thirties with tattoos and perfectly styled hair and clothes. Alberta, who was a gorgeous girl with caramel skin and amber eyes, was maybe into her thirties. And Sooz, her girlfriend, who had short spiky hair and was also heavily tattooed. There were also three younger guys outside Gemma could see them in the backyard talking to Scott. She figured that was Tom, Trent and Nick, that Janine had mentioned earlier, she could also see Daniel and Ryan at the grill, Gemma had met the restaurant manager once before, but only in passing from Marshside Mama's.

It didn't take Gemma long to realize that everyone knew each other from work and partying together. She felt like she definitely was not one of the cool kids. It was a weird and strange feeling, one she had experienced a long, long time ago, way back in high school, which was so long ago it took her a second to figure it out. She also felt like everyone's disapproving big sister, from the snippets of conversation she heard, it was so superficial and immature! She was aware of not actually wanting to know these people or even be part of their scene. It felt like a continuation of high school/college. She realized she didn't have much of an option; however, if this was her husband's scene, she should make an effort to at least be liked by these people. She plastered on a grin and thought she better make the most of it.

"Hi, Gemma!" Daniel beamed at her as he came in from the backyard with a plate full of food straight from the grill. He put down the plate and gave her one of those superficial "we're friends" hugs, which she actually appreciated. She wondered if her doubt and intimidation was written all over her face.

Daniel smelled like a mixture of barbeque, alcohol, and men's cologne.

Where was Scott? He never used to just ditch her at parties. He would always be right next to her, introducing her to everyone, so proud that she was his wife. *Not today, not anymore*, she thought, momentarily feeling a wave of isolation and bitterness wash over her.

Wow, even Noah has fitted in perfectly. Well, that was a relief. Being an only child, she often worried if he was a little too satisfied with being on his own. She had often wished that he had a younger sibling. He used to ask for one all the time when he was around four and five. She and Scott had discussed it shortly before they moved, before he was offered his "big promotion." He said he didn't think he was ready. They didn't have very good health insurance (and being a cosmetics salesperson/makeup artist didn't provide any healthcare options as she worked an average of two hours shy of being "full time," so they were not obliged to offer any benefits) that if there was any type of hiccup or problem with the pregnancy, especially since she was over forty, or a problem with the baby, they would not be able to handle it. They were finally starting to make headway with their financial situation, and she agreed. It was logical, but Gemma was crushed at the time. She was already forty-two then. She knew her fertility was limited although she had always believed Scott when he had said that by the time Noah was five, "we'd be a four-member family."

In retrospect, Gemma thought she should have just "accidentally" gotten pregnant as a "surprise." It seemed to work (from the outside) for so many other couples she had seen, but she wasn't the sort of woman to pull that one and always believed that if there was a decision affecting the whole family (and their finances), then the whole family should be in support. But still…

"Hey, need a glass of wine?" Janine's voice broke into her thoughts. "Looks like you're totally spacing out there." She had two glasses of white wine, one in each hand. They were those stemless wine glasses that Gemma liked, and she gratefully took one that was held out to her. Janine continued, "I'm cooking some hot dogs for the kids, as well as mac and cheese and corn on the cob. Is Noah good with that?"

"Sure," answered Gemma taking a sip. It was a sweet cold white wine—not normally what Gemma drank, but hey, when in Rome, right? It was kind of nice for someone else to take charge of dinner for Noah for a change too.

"No problem," Janine replied. "Food's almost done for them, ours isn't too far behind."

Gemma nodded. "I always like to get the kids fed and sorted first anyway."

Janine smiled at her and walked back into the kitchen, calling behind her, "Don't be shy, come into the kitchen. We can chat."

Gemma followed, feeling a little less awkward. Maybe she had read Janine all wrong. Maybe Scott was right, we could be friends. She took another mouthful of wine.

Gemma walked into the kitchen, well, to the kitchen entryway. It was a small L-shaped kitchen, and Daniel was already in there, pulling stuff out of the pantry, and Thomas, was darting around trying to grab food off the counters, Daniel was swatting at his little hand. Also, one of the younger guys Gemma had seen outside, was at the fridge grabbing some beers, tucking them under his arm. He looked at her and introduced himself. "Hi, I'm Trent." He smiled a charming flashy smile. "Did I see you come in with Scott?"

Gemma smiled. "Yes, you did, and our son Noah."

"Yeah," he said, looking her up and down in an oddly personal way. "I met him outside with Scott." He went on. "He's cute, like you," he said appreciatively, giving her a wink.

"Geez, Trent!" Janine butted in. "Way to hit on the boss's wife!" Janine elbowed him as he walked past, and he almost dropped one of the five beer cans he was balancing.

He shrugged his shoulders and laughed. "What do you expect?" he said to Janine. He winked at Gemma as he walked by.

Janine scoffed. "Don't worry about him," she said. "He's harmless!" she yelled at his back as he walked through the living room on his way outside. She realized she hadn't even told him her name. She wondered with a flash of pride if it was because Scott may have mentioned her before or Trent really didn't care what her name was and just knew she was Scott's wife. Well, that was a strange feeling. She had always been used to being in the partnership—Gemma and Scott, Scott and Gemma. It had taken her ages to get used to being thought of as just "Noah's mom," now she had to get used to just "Scott's wife" too? Huh.

Still, she was flattered. Sizing him up, she realized he was probably only about twenty-three or twenty-four.

Gemma suddenly felt a little self-conscious. She hadn't really thought about what she was wearing or that she needed to dress up or anything. Her dark hair was relatively natural compared to the crew around her, and she was wearing her usual weekend "uniform"—a form-fitting black t-shirt, skinny three-quarter-length jeans, and ballet flats. She wasn't one to spend hours fussing about her clothes. She knew what worked for her and stuck to that. It worked. Her makeup was natural and flattering. Again, she didn't like to look like she spent hours on herself. She had to commit to a full face of makeup every day she worked. There was no way she would do that by choice on her days off. Good grief, she had other things to do! But looking around her, these people liked to be the center of attention. The girls all seemed to be dressed to outdo each other, their makeup alone was completely overdone for a weekend cookout. Most of them were wearing workout clothes or stylishly torn jeans and tight t-shirts. Gemma knew the restaurant uniform was a white shirt and black tie for everyone, so maybe this was their release, she rationalized to herself. She also wondered if any of them knew what she did for work. Most of them looked like they painted their clothes on. Gemma wasn't embarrassed for them, she was no prude, but *wow, have some decency people*. She laughed to herself, observing once more, how judgmental she could be when feeling left out. She threw back the last mouthful of wine in an attempt to change her thoughts.

She suddenly felt completely irrelevant and "out of the loop." She knew she looked at least ten years younger than she was, but this whole aging woman thing was tough! Age is not kind to women! At work, she came across so many women who were angry and bitter that they felt they were being overlooked, that men of their age group just clamored for the younger (often stupider) girls. Gemma always did her best to build these women up, never really understanding why they were so angry. She truly believed women aged like fine wine, gradually trading the beauty of youth for a more graceful wise persona, but for the first time she understood that view. She knew it—geez, the whole industry she worked in preyed on women's insecurities, she knew that, too. She had always seen it. But until this moment, she had never actually felt how badly it stung—especially being surrounded by all the beautiful people.

She realized she had tuned out and that Janine was saying something to her. She was looking at her with a strange look on her face. "Sorry," Gemma spoke, "what were you saying?"

Janine handed her a bowl of salad to put on the counter beside her. "I said don't let Trent upset you, he tries it on everyone."

Gemma laughed, surprised that Janine had thought she was disturbed by a younger guy flirting with her. "Actually," Gemma started, "I thought it was sweet."

"Sweet, ha." Janine laughed. "He'll be offended that you thought it was sweet. I don't think that's what he was going for."

Gemma took the bottle of wine Janine handed her and poured more into her glass and took another mouthful. Janine went on. "Trent's claim to fame is being the first one to get with any new staff members, if you know what I mean." Janine gave her a knowing look, like she was sharing the biggest secret ever. Gemma nearly spat out her wine, she couldn't quite hold in the laugh.

"That doesn't strike me as anything to be proud of." She regained control. Obviously the old moniker "don't screw the crew" was not adhered to in this workplace. She realized Janine was staring blankly at her. Suddenly awkward, Gemma thought Janine had absolutely no concept of sarcasm. She quickly changed the subject. "Do you want more wine?" Gemma held up the bottle toward Janine's almost empty glass. Janine seemed happy to comply and picked up her glass so she could fill it up.

After that interaction, Gemma decided to head outside to see what Scott was up to with a mental note that Janine was not the sarcastic type. He saw her come out but was in mid-story and barely acknowledged she was there, except to angle himself slightly toward her. Gemma dutifully stood next to him, waiting for him to finish and introduce her to the group he was standing with. She could feel their eyes all over her. She wondered what he'd said about her, or if he'd said anything at all. She almost felt homesick for where they had lived before. Everyone knew them—Scott and Gemma, Gemma and Scott. She felt secure in her place as his wife, next to him, supporting him. Everyone knew they had always been together and always would be. She felt respected—not like here. She felt like nothing here, no one, just another face in the crowd. That kind of pissed her off, although she didn't know how she felt. Irrelevant? Lost? Invisible? All strange and new feelings, she was having trouble defining them herself. And that felt awful.

Suddenly the man who was such a huge part of her, who had built her up and done life with her, who had made her feel so valid as a person and woman, was not interested in her anymore. Well, that was how it felt. Watching him being the star of the show, she wondered if he even wanted her there at the party or at all. She could see that everyone looked up to him, which was good. You'd hope that everyone you're in charge of respected and listened to you.

Scott finished his story and turned to her. "How are you doing, Gemma? Do you know everyone here?" he said, motioning to the group. There was Daniel, Trent, and another guy she hadn't met yet.

"No." She smiled shyly at everyone.

Scott put his arm around her waist and guided her closer to him. "Okay, well you know Daniel."

She nodded. *Not as well as you do*, she thought. "Hi."

Daniel gave her a big smile, and she instantly felt more comfortable.

"This is Trent." Trent gave her a butter-wouldn't-melt-in-his-mouth look.

"Yeah, I met him in the kitchen." Gemma smiled back. "Hello, again."

"And this is Tom." Scott nodded in Tom's direction. He also was very good looking and obviously worked out as well. His hair was in a man bun, and his t-shirt was very tight.

"Hi." Tom nodded.

"Nice to meet you." Gemma smiled at him too, impressed at how normal and polite he was.

Gemma hung outside for a little while, barely involved in the conversation, listening and pretending to be interested in the things they talked about, joining in here and there to be polite, continually glancing at Scott hoping he would bring her in to the conversation like he always did when he could see that she was hanging back, but it was almost like they were so involved in their own lives and stories, their fantasy football league, who was playing what team when, who was going to the game next month, who got drunk when and with who, who bedded who, who was at brunch last week (apparently Scott was, although he had failed to mention anything to Gemma. She was sure he said he had to work a double that day). Nobody was interested in hearing anything she had to say about anything. She studied her wine glass after each sip. It didn't taste so sweet now.

It was about then that Gemma noticed Scott was not wearing his wedding ring.

She felt a bit stunned. How long had it been off his finger? She could still see the indent from wearing it for nearly two decades. Maybe something happened to it?

She knew he was a "hands-on" type of manager who had no issue jumping in to help as necessary, who knew?

Scott felt her inquisitive look and glanced at her while subconsciously shoving his hand deep into his pocket. Gemma felt a little smug that they were still so obviously connected. Previously she could be thinking about him, and he would call or look over at her or give her a kiss on the forehead or a smile or something that made her feel like she was his. Now that he didn't do that, she felt like he didn't even want to be seen with her or Noah, like they cramped his style. Gemma shook her head in an attempt to get rid of that crazy thought. Scott loved them. He was just so busy with his job, wasn't he? She momentarily felt awful—again. Gemma thought she should stop drinking, she wasn't liking these feelings or thoughts she was having.

Inside, she could see Janine had the kids sitting at the table eating and felt very hungry herself.

Gemma asked if Daniel wanted her to take in the platter of hamburgers he had just removed from the grill. "That'd be great," he said, giving her a sly wink.

Okay, Gemma thought to herself as she went to the door, *that was weird*. As she walked back in the house, everyone was talking to each other. No one even looked at her. She felt like such a misfit in this group. This whole thing was so weird. Obviously, "these cool kids" were an exclusive bunch and didn't see the need to include someone who didn't work with them.

For a brief moment, painfully shy Gemma felt like just keeping on going, straight out the door and away from this strange scene. Although it had been a while since "Gemma the introvert" had really even had a look-in on her life, just fleeting glimpses here and there; being Mom to Noah and working in people's personal spaces had really made her get over it and find ways to feel comfortable in social settings. For a long time, she'd used drugs and alcohol—not excessively, just enough to relax her anxiety—to get over herself, but after finding out she was pregnant with Noah, she realized she would have to find other ways to overcome any social anxiety she experienced, and she was happy to have the perspective that she now had, away from the party scene. Scott was understanding too, always just there for her.

Or he had been, she corrected herself again.

Which is why she was so miffed by this deal. She knew what was up. Until nine years ago, she was one of them, or at least part of the group, but firmly attached to Scott, secure in her place in the world, and there seemed to be a lot more friendly joking around and welcoming atmosphere in her memory than this (although there had been no kids running around). She totally recognized the stereotypes and the games these people played, which was fine, just not what she was into anymore! Good grief, she was happy to not be participating in the dramas of the egocentric hospitality world. Did they even know what stereotypes they were? Did they even care? She questioned the feeling that she was supposed to prove herself or something.

The platter was taken out of her hands by Janine with a "Thanks, babe. Grab yourself a plate! Food's pretty much all here," as she didn't even look at her.

"Awesome," replied Gemma. She took a plate and filled it up in the kitchen that was bustling with activity. No one said anything to her, and she was at a loss as to what to say to anyone.

"Wow, it all looks so good," she said out loud to no one in particular. Nobody even acknowledged they'd heard her. *All righty…*

As she came around the corner, she saw an empty chair at the table with the kids. Noah saw her. "Sit over here, Mom!" He excitedly patted the seat next to him.

Gemma was relieved to feel wanted and gave him a big smile. "Of course, buddy." She kissed him on the head as she plopped down next to him.

At the table, she chatted with the kids and couldn't help but notice all the other adults came inside to get their food and head back outside. Soon Gemma was the only adult still inside, at the table, with the kids. Someone closed the door to the patio, and Gemma didn't know whether she was supposed to take that personally or not. Obviously the gang was all there. Huh. Way to make the newcomer feel welcome.

She didn't see Scott come in to grab food. Actually, she couldn't see him at all.

Gemma looked at her watch. Well, this officially sucked. She was tired and over making excuses for these people. The wine had gone directly to her head, and she just wanted to go home.

"All right, Noah, shall we head home after this?"

Noah nodded. He was mashing the remnants of his meal into a flat pile. Zoe and Thomas got up from the table and sat on the couch. Erin went over as well, all just leaving everything on the table. *I guess they don't have to ask to be excused or put up their plates or anything.* "I'm done, Mom, can we go?"

Gemma nodded. "Let's find Dad and see if he wants to come too."

Noah looked disappointed. "Isn't he coming home with us?"

"I don't know, son, let's ask." Gemma tried to sound hopeful.

They walked over to the sliding glass door. Gemma could see Scott still standing by the grill surrounded by Jacob, Ashley, Sooz, Janine, Daniel, and Kelly. It looked like they had just done a round of shots—again. *Great*, Gemma thought to herself.

They stepped out, and Gemma immediately smelt the pungent aroma of marijuana. She scanned everyone quickly to see where and who was smoking that. She glanced down quickly to see if Noah had noticed. He was seemingly oblivious. Just at the corner of the house, she could see Trent and Tom smoking a joint.

They saw her step out with Noah and disappeared further around the corner out of sight. The smoke was still pluming out from around the corner though. Gemma nearly laughed out loud. *Stupid kids*, she thought to herself.

She walked over to where Scott was and kind of wiggled herself in as nobody moved. "Honey, have you had anything to eat?" She noticed he looked pretty drunk, although she was sure no one else probably noticed seeing as they didn't know him as well as she did. Scott was very good at being a sober acting drunk. Gemma figured it was probably from his lifetime's experience of drinking and all the role models that had remained drunk through his childhood.

He attempted to focus on her for a second. "It's okay, babe, you don't have to act like my mother. I can look after myself, thanks." As he finished his sentence, he looked to the others as he took a swig from his bottle. *For what, approval?* Gemma thought she heard muffled laughs. She felt her face burning. She felt wounded and completely deflated, like someone had just taken the air out of her. *Was he serious right now?* Why did she suddenly feel like she was in high school again? There was no way she was going to let anyone here see his drunken bravado affect her.

"Cool, well, we're going home." Gemma searched his face for her Scott, but he wasn't there. It was buzzed Scott.

"All right, I don't know when I'll be there. Maybe soon." She was aware that everyone was standing there watching and listening to their conversation. She suddenly felt irritated and worthless.

Noah stepped forward. "Come home with us, Dad! Please," he pleaded and pulled at Scott's shirt.

Scott removed the little boy's hand, with what…embarrassment? Gemma didn't like his attitude toward Noah right now or toward her for that matter. "I'll be home soon, son."

Noah just turned and took his mom's hand, not even surprised. He didn't seem to notice his dad's ambivalence toward him, but she sure did. It felt like she had just been punched in the solar plexus. Gemma took a deliberate breath to regain her composure.

"Don't worry, Gemma, we'll make sure he gets something to eat," Janine volunteered. Again, no eye contact, not even a nod as she spoke to her. *That was weird.*

"Fine, didn't mean to cramp your style or anything there, hotshot," said Gemma curtly. "We'll see ourselves out." She took Noah's hand as she spun around, feeling the tears welling up in her eyes, and went to walk down the side of the house but remembered the potheads and changed direction to go back through the house.

"Gem!" Scott called after her. She was not interested in what he had to say, and she was about to start crying. If she even looked at him right now, she would fall apart. *What just happened? How could he be so hurtful and horrible? Did he secretly hate them? Was he embarrassed to be seen with them?* The awful feeling in her solar plexus had moved to her throat. She felt she could hardly breathe. Gemma managed to get out the front door and halfway down the driveway before she let the tears fall.

"Wait, Mom," Noah said, trying to catch up. He grabbed her hand. "Why was Dad so mean to you?"

"I don't know, honey." Gemma was aware she still didn't want Noah to think badly of his dad. *WTF?* she thought to herself. She took a deep breath and changed the subject. This wasn't something she wanted to dump on him. "How about some dessert when we get home? Rice pudding?" She knew it was one of Noah's favorites.

"Oh yes, please!" Noah ran ahead of her, excited. She wiped her eyes, and by the time they got across the road and back to their house, she had pulled herself together enough to start thinking about the things that had to be done to prepare for the next day, but first, dessert.

She and Noah sat on the couch with their rice pudding and talked about the new friends he had made. He really liked Thomas and Zoe and was so happy to have some friends on the street. Gemma silently wished she felt the same way. She just felt left out and had a sinking feeling deep inside. Like she wasn't included in the group of cool kids, because, she wasn't considered one of them. *Oh boy, this sucked!* Being into her forties, she never imagined in her wildest dreams that this is what she'd be dealing with. She was grateful when it was time to get Noah into the shower.

Gemma unloaded the dishwasher and fed Gary, she sat down on the floor and patted him while he ate. He purred while he was chewing. She smiled to herself. He was the most content and happy cat she'd ever owned. At times like this, when he was just there with his deep purr and observant green eyes, making everything seem normal and calm, she couldn't help but wonder if he was a gift from God himself.

*****

He was just a tiny kitten she and Scott had found in a dumpster behind a strip mall as they were riding their bikes to a playground one fall afternoon when Noah was about three. Gemma thought she had heard a faint meow as they cycled through the parking lot, but Scott hadn't heard it, and they kept going. Gemma had thought about it the whole time at the playground, however, and an hour or so later on the way back past, she had made them stop. This time, Noah had heard it too. He kept pointing at the dumpster and mimicking the plaintive cry.

"Just let me look, it'll only take a second," Gemma had said before Scott could protest. She slid the door of the dumpster open and peered into the dim interior. There was definitely a kitten in there! She could see him in the back corner next to some garbage bags. His meow was weaker and so pitiful, she leaned all the way in to try and coax him over the where she could reach. He was timid and not cooperating.

As she had stepped back to leverage herself to climb in, Scott stopped her. He was right there. "Stop, honey, I'll get in there. There's no need for you to get in a dumpster!" He kissed the top of her head. "I have to take a shower and work later anyway."

"How chivalrous of you, kind sir." She stepped back and gave him a courtesy.

He winked at her as he climbed into the dumpster. Noah laughed and clapped his hands. He was still strapped into the trailer behind the bike Scott had been riding, watching everything. As soon as Scott got into the dumpster, the kitten scooted over to the over side with a hiss.

Gemma tried to make soothing noises and give guidance at the same time. "Try talking softly to him, honey. I bet he's terrified."

Scott laughed. "How do you know it's a he?" Scott asked, attempting to grab him again.

"I don't know, it just looks like a boy."

Scott gave her an "okay, sweetheart" look over his shoulder. He was used to her offbeat hunches that always turned out to be right. Luckily, the dumpster was not too full with only half a dozen or so trash bags haphazardly in there, but it stunk like a dumpster. Gemma was grateful Scott had volunteered to get in. He did his best to not stand on any trash while trying to scoop up the tiny kitten, but of course, that was impossible. After a couple of tries and some soothing noises from Scott, the kitten seemed to give up and just stopped and gave a halfhearted hiss as Scott picked him up. He was grey and white with dirty smudges and big dirty feet and big green eyes. As he passed him out to her, Gemma could already hear him purring. His tiny body trembled with the giant purr from within. He wasn't in too terrible condition, all things considered. No fleas or ticks. And definitely a boy.

Gemma put him in the backpack she had on. It had hardly anything in it except for a couple of sunhats and their empty lunch bag. The kitten didn't protest and seemed happy to snuggle into somewhere warm and dark. "What shall we call him?" she asked Scott and Noah.

"Gary!" they both replied.

Gemma smiled to herself. Scott and Gemma had been fans of SpongeBob for a long time, and Noah (by default) was a fan too. He would giggle uncontrollably whenever Gary, who was SpongeBob's pet snail, would meow like a cat. From that day, Gary was a faithful friend and companion to the whole family. He was family, Noah's buddy and bedtime guardian, Scott's late night pal, her own friend and sweet companion, often just sitting close enough to watch what she was doing and purr—his big, contented, reassuring, calming purr.

*****

Gemma woke at 2:30 a.m. Scott was not in bed, *was he even home?* She went out to the living room. He was passed out on the couch in the fetal position, shoes on and everything, Gemma sighed and stood there, looking at him for a long time, feeling a mixture of pity, disappointment, and sadness. She sighed again. Ever the devoted wife, she took his shoes off and put them on the floor. *What was he doing? How did he think this was okay?* Her Scott from before would never fall asleep fully clothed on the couch. He always had pride in being able to keep it together enough to get himself into bed—with his wife.

She got the throw blanket from the shelf and put it over him and knelt down next to the couch, put her arms around him, and buried her face into his neck. "I love you, Scott Harris. Come back to me, remember us."

In his drunken stupor, he wrapped his arms around her like he used to and muttered something incoherent. Gemma brushed away the tears as she eased out of his grip and went back to bed. *What was happening?* She felt like she was losing him and their marriage. Because she was.

PART 2

Is God Listening?

Chapter 7

Grief and Memories

We humans are basically ever hopeful creatures and cling to the good times and good memories, even when everything is falling apart right in front of our eyes, even when offered irrefutable proof that those times have gone—and are never coming back. Somehow we keep going, scraping through every day, silently yearning for the sun to shine on our lives once more, lifting us, propelling us forward.

*****

Since the first time she met Scott, Gemma had known he was her human. She used to silently scoff at stories she heard from other women of all ages who would say, "I knew he was the one." But after meeting Scott for the first time, she knew it to be true. They had met by chance at a postproduction party she was attending at a bar where he worked. He was instantly smitten and asked her out the next night. They felt like they had known each other for ever and planned a trip to Mexico right on the first date. They were inseparable after that night. Both had felt so confident in their union, they got married five months after that first date. Nobody was surprised or protested, it was always the easiest most natural thing in the world. They shared the same dark humor and thought outside the box, they were each other's perfect mirrors in so many ways yet complemented each other as well. She was somewhat shy and introverted outside of her work environment, he was extroverted and thrived being part of the crowd. They admired and respected each other and had made a great team. She was his "partner-in-crime." And physically, they were one. Sex had always been amazing. They had both likened it to out-of-body experiences. Neither had ever had such chemistry or compatibility with anyone else nor did they want to. They would lay awake at night and talk for hours, wrapped up in each other, not knowing where one ended and the other began.

During the first twelve or so years of their relationship, they had worked and saved and travelled together. From that first trip to Mexico, they had backpacked around Europe, hiked and camped in the mountains of Colorado during the summer, partied in Las Vegas several times, spent three summers working and playing in Martha's Vineyard and a couple of winters working and snowboarding in Utah. Each happy and complete in the other's company, wherever they were together was home. In love and inspired by each other, they did their best to fly under the radar wherever possible. The only person they ever spoke to about their relationship was each other. It was all as it should be. Gemma never really understood why so many women talked to everyone else about their relationships and not the person they were in the relationship with.

Scott had never been so communicative with a woman before. Gemma was so easy to talk to, they could communicate with each other about anything and everything. And they did.

Scott and Gemma. Gemma and Scott. Mr. and Mrs. Harris. Together forever to love one another.

They would talk about how grateful they felt that they had found each other and could just focus on their lives together, joking how they would be as old people—that horny old couple at the rest home. They learned from each other and taught each other what it felt like to be loved completely and unconditionally, what it was like to have a champion, a supporter, someone to build you up and keep you grounded.

Scott had a great sense of humor and would make her laugh so much, she'd be doubled over crying. She'd crack him up too. She would call him at work and prank call him in different voices. He'd call her to say goodnight and sing her corny old showtime songs.

Gemma had never felt so full and loved. Neither had Scott. She was an amazing woman who kept up with him mentally and, if anything, was one step ahead of him at times. He loved the challenge. She made him want to be a better person. He made her want to be more—more true to herself, more open, more brave. He encouraged her to learn the things she had always wanted to learn—how to ride a motorbike, snowboard, surf, and play the ukulele (not all at the same time). He told her more than once that she had saved his life, saved him from the drunk single gigolo bartending life that he was sick of and had wanted more for quite some time. All the girls he had previously dated or bed (or both) were empty, vapid stupid girls he just wasn't in to. He had almost resigned himself to that. She believed him.

She loved the way he cherished her, treated her as his equal. Every other guy had talked at her, not to her. She loved how she felt when she was with him. He felt like he had hit the jackpot; she was smart, beautiful, strong, funny, creative, inspiring, and sexy as hell.

Sure they had their ups and downs. A couple of times, they had to have serious conversations with each other about the amount of partying they were doing and how, if they weren't careful, it could all easily slip out of control, but they never missed work and always paid their rent and bills and made their next travel goals. With each other's strength and support, they kept a balance on things. When she was weak, he was strong, and vice versa. They would lay in bed and talk and make love for hours. Sometimes they would talk until dawn, finally falling asleep in each other's arms. Gemma had always known Scott was very social, but he managed to keep his drinking under control so she never really gave it too much thought. When she was concerned and would say something, he would agree and dial it back. He liked to be at home with Gemma, cooking dinner together or playing chess and drinking a bottle of wine. Sometimes they would invite friends over and cook for them too. It was always Scott and Gemma, Gemma and Scott. They had no secrets and knew the depths of each other's souls—darkness and light. Everything.

Although they had talked about what they would do "after the next travel adventure," it was Scott that first suggested they consider their next adventure be to start a family and stay put for a time while he worked his way into management with Marshside Mama's. Gemma was happy to oblige; it felt like the next natural step in their journey together.

She got pregnant almost instantly, which was more of a surprise to her than him. Her pregnancy was easy and trouble-free. They knew they were having a boy early on, and Noah was born after a quick six-hour labor. He was a happy, chill baby who fitted perfectly into their lives and bought so much joy and love, with his big brown eyes and infectious giggle. Gemma easily took to motherhood. Scott needed some encouragement here and there, but he was always keen to jump in even if he had no idea what he was doing. He was a thoughtful and considerate dad. When he was aware that Gemma needed a break, he would take the baby and let her nap.

When Noah was about one, Scott accepted his first management position. He had been working for the restaurant for a while and received so much support from the owners and upper management, it too felt like the next natural step. Although he had so much more responsibility, and his nights were later, they took it all in stride.

As long as they had each other, they could do anything. With his new reliable income, Gemma could just work part time, and pick up the occasional wedding makeup job from her wedding planner friends.

Sometimes they got frustrated with each other but still managed to have day trips or nights away so they kept close. Often Gemma would wake up at 1:00 or 2:00 a.m. as he was getting home, and they would talk about his work, the people, and situations he dealt with. They would get a sitter every few weeks so he could take her out and they could "be adults" together. They always managed to talk things out, and their communication was as strong as ever.

Life was good.

Gemma was secure in the knowledge that their relationship had a solid base, and now they all they needed to do was maintain and keep building their plans into fruition. They had been through so much together. Again, it just seemed like natural progression.

These memories were so fresh, Gemma could not let them go. There had to be some way to bring back Scott and their relationship the way it used to be, hadn't there?

Someone just can't completely change everything they ever were…can they? Can alcohol do that? Can it take away someone's compassion, empathy, consideration, and their ability to tune into another person? Sometimes after a particularly big partying weekend, Gemma would joke with Scott that he was brain damaged from all the partying because sometimes it actually seemed like he was stupider when he was hungover. Scott would be good natured about it, neither of them were very concerned. She couldn't really find any definitive information as to whether or not drinking excessively destroyed IQ. Or was she completely delusional the whole time?

Little by little, things got difficult. It was harder and harder to clearly communicate with Scott. Real life kicked in, and they lost their way. Scott seemed less and less like the Scott Gemma knew. When he would decline to commit to decisions or take action on things within their family unit or around the house, she put it down to him being so busy at work. She found herself taking responsibility for so much around the house and making decisions to do with their lives, Noah, and their financial life—things Scott wasn't even interested in having conversations about. He'd make promises to talk about it on his next night/day/afternoon/weekend off, but something always came up. She would get frustrated and try to talk to him, he would just blow her off. Didn't he get it? Some things could not wait!

When he wouldn't get out of bed to do promised activities with her and Noah, she would make excuses to herself and Noah. He'd never admit he was hungover, but she knew he was.

Gemma was aware of the passing of days, weeks, and months with so much left undone.

Scott never had time for them anymore. She couldn't help but notice though he always made time for everyone else—someone's birthday, last day, visit, new to town, leaving a job, stag do, hen's party, retirement, winning team, good day, bad day, twenty-first, thirtieth, fortieth, fiftieth, you name it. Always an excuse to drink and be out.

When Gemma would point out that he was forgetting about her and Noah, he would acknowledge that he had been neglectful and genuinely make an effort for a week or two, so it was easy to forgive and move on. At first, he seemed concerned, and he would seriously make an effort to make it up to her and Noah—cook dinner, or buy her flowers, plan a family day trip somewhere. She would be temporarily placated with his genuine remorse and be happy to do what she could to keep their home and lives running smoothly.

As time wore on, however, he made less and less effort and turned away more often. When she would say something, he'd get impatient with her and tell that she was always so negative. She'd get angry that he wouldn't even try to listen. Almost like he didn't even care about her thoughts and feelings anymore.

It was like she was speaking another language.

Gemma felt she could be telling him the house was on fire, and he'd go ahead and call a plumber.

It slowly dawned on her that he was treating her the way he always said he never would, just like his father had treated his mother—as "the wife" and not recognizing her, Gemma the person. Just the "wife and mother of their child," like somehow in his mind she had given up all entitlement to feel and be treated like his equal anymore. She didn't need time off or a break, she didn't need anyone to take care of her, and her asking for that meant she was being needy and negative. Somehow working thirty-eight hours a week and being main caregiver to Noah, and house keeper, and accountant, and never able to spend time doing what she wanted and collapsing into bed exhausted every night without even a spare moment to breathe, was supposed to be some sort of privilege.

This made Gemma simultaneously sad and angry. He would say that he still loved her and wanted them to be together. But he didn't act like it.

She tried everything she could think of and read about online. Those oh-so-helpful but inadvertently demeaning "How to Be a

Better Girl for Your Guy" articles, the ones about being sexier, more understanding, helpful, not complaining, not repeating herself, not nagging, handling it all on her own, making an effort to be happy to see him every time no matter what, keeping their expenses low, not having too much debt or overhead commitments—all of which she hated. It felt so fake and artificial! How had they somehow regressed into the 1950s?

This wasn't what they'd spent the last fifteen or sixteen years working for! Or at all what she expected.

And to top it all off, she was watching her body and her looks change with age (because *age is so hard on women*). Her man, her husband, was distancing himself from her more and more every day/week/month. For a brief moment, she thought about being down on herself for aging but couldn't really follow through with *that* line of thought.

She was more at peace with herself and her body than she ever had been. Scott had been instrumental in building her courage and self-worth. There was no way she was giving that up.

She was weary though.

Very occasionally when she just felt like completely giving up, he would get up early and make them breakfast or do some other totally unexpected small action that let her see he *was* still there, and he *did* care. Or she would think she saw that.

This would keep her going for another week or so, until she would be back to that same place—alone, frustrated, lonely, and no way to communicate or find the right words to say so that he would hear. She had really presumed that child rearing with Scott would be as much of a wonderful adventure as their married life had been so far, and for a while, it was. But the reality of raising a human seemed to make Scott want to escape any way he could and not feel any obligation to his wife or son.

Gemma knew Scott's family dynamic. She rationalized that this was obviously his family model. Although previously, when they would talk about his childhood and his parents' marriage and subsequent remarriages, especially his father's (who had since been married five times), he would always say he would "never turn out like his father." But he had never really made a conscious effort beyond saying the words to ensure he did not turn out that way. She knew her own family model had been dysfunctional and made a continual conscious effort to be super aware of her own habits and parenting. When she caught herself being impatient and yelling, she would stop and even apologize to Noah. She read books and had talked to her friends about being a different mother to the one she had grown up with, and she never ever called him names or hit him—ever.

Gemma was happy with her progress as a mother. The way she felt about her progress as wife in a supportive marital relationship, however, was dismal. She read book after book, looking for answers, never wanting to be stuck in the same problems she was always looking for a way to fix things. Even in counseling, she was the one bringing up the ideas and theories at home the counselor had spoken with them about. It was during one of these conversations that Scott had let it slip that he was "only going to counselling because she was the messed up one. Once she had her head sorted out, they would be fine." She gave up making them go to counselling after that revelation. *After six months of going to counselling usually once a week, this is all he came up with? Wow.*

How do you fix this? How does a person become so different? How do they completely change without ever showing the slightest indication of their potential flip in the previous decade and a half or so? Gemma spent hours in the dark and lonely nights, going over every memory, moment, situation, looking for an indication that she had missed somehow. *Was she a total fool? Completely blind the whole time?* No. She knew she wasn't. There had been no early warning of what was to come. So he liked to drink, everyday. At least a couple of beers or a bottle of wine, it was never really a problem, it was just something he did.

When she would bring it up, Scott didn't understand the problem. "Other couples are like this. Other husbands drink every day. It's just a couple of beers after work. What's your problem?" he would ask, challenging her.

Gemma would feel frustrated, questioning her own perception of the situation. "We have never been like other couples!" she would fire back.

Still, he was her man, her husband. She truly believed that it was her place to love him continually, unconditionally. She still held true to her belief that they were supposed to be together forever.

One man for one woman, through thick and thin. So things were a little thin at the moment. She had always thought that referred to finances, not the actual *relating* to each other part.

Very rarely, he would still listen to her pour out her soul, all her fears about the direction of their relationship—where it was headed, what was going to happen as Noah grew older—which she appreciated, but instead of feeling validated or heard by her biggest champion, like she used to, she couldn't help but notice he would have nothing to say—no thoughts or fears to share himself. She would ask him questions to try and figure out where he was with everything, but he would just shrug in a noncommittal way. She would end the conversation feeling miffed. At first Gemma would get upset and cry, pleading for some sort of response from him, which grew into frustration, and she would push him for an answer or something. It was almost like he didn't mind or see what was happening or even worse, acted as if it had nothing to do with him. Like he had just "opted out" of participating in their life, as if he had already "done his time" and so didn't have to put any more in.

Gemma was confused by this. She also knew that alcohol had so much to do with it. She wrote herself a poem one day. "My husband has a mistress, her name is alcohol, and he will come running, whenever she does call."

But she never finished it. She had always known he was stronger than any pull of any addiction—or thought he was. With her help, together, they could conquer anything! They were such a potent team when they held a singular vision. She doubted that belief more and more as time wore on.

Chapter 8

Finding Comfort in Uncomfortable Places

Over time, she had read as much as she could about alcoholics and alcoholism. She was no dummy. In the course of her life, work, and travels, she had met plenty of "functioning alcoholics." Honestly, it seemed almost every single man she knew or had known (family, friends, coworkers, customers, and acquaintances) of all ages had some dependence on alcohol in some form or other. Scott's whole family were drinkers and partiers from way back. His brothers, sister, both his parents and their past and current spouses, all drank excessively and, as far as she could tell, always had. Everything she read about alcoholics and alcoholism didn't really seem to fit him though. He wasn't abusive or slovenly, he still took pride in his appearance, he was never late for work, he had a great work ethic, he didn't usually drink alone or try to hide it, he didn't have any run-ins with the law, he wasn't outwardly depressed, he didn't lie about his drinking, and he wasn't a sloppy drunk. In fact, it was only that she knew him so well she could tell how wasted he was. She honestly didn't think anyone else really noticed—or cared to notice. He did drink a lot, he always had, always. Like daily, at least two or three beers or more, as well as the shots of whatever liquor he fancied—sometimes whiskey, sometimes tequila or vodka. She really wasn't sure that she believed Scott had a disease. She really did think he could stop whenever he wanted, he just didn't want to. He didn't think he needed to. *Was he using it to escape something? What, her? His family? Why? Did he have a problem with his drinking?* She often wondered if her focusing on it was making it worse…

Which is why, when one of her customers commented in passing (and not at all directed at her) that going to Al-Anon was the "best thing she had ever done," Gemma seriously looked into going to a meeting—which is all she did for a few weeks. Looked into it, checked the schedules online, read reviews of the venue where the meetings were held. She couldn't find any actual reviews of the meetings or anything though. It seemed very secretive, almost clandestine. Although she didn't really feel like yelling from the rooftops that her husband had a drinking problem, somehow, she felt it made her look like a terrible wife.

However much she reasoned with herself not to go, she knew she should at least check it out. There was no point in denying herself some sort of help or perspective—or something.

As luck would have it, there was a regular meeting (actually a bunch of them) right in town, not too far from where she worked. She spent a few evenings driving by the building to get familiar with where it was. Finally she could put it off no longer. There was a meeting the next night Scott was off, so Gemma decided she would go. She let him know a few days before so he would be home for Noah. He asked where she was going.

"To a meeting," she replied. "I'll be about an hour." He didn't even ask what sort of meeting. Although to be fair, over the years, she had gone to plenty of meetings or trainings for work or Noah's sports or school. He used to be interested or pretend to be. He barely even registered interest these days.

When the time came and she was getting ready to leave, he asked, "How long will you be?" He turned to look at her, his chocolate brown eyes searching hers for a moment. *Wow he never looks at me anymore.* She gave him a half smile.

"About an hour, I think. Please make sure Noah has had a shower and is in bed by seven thirty."

Fat chance that'll happen, she thought to herself as she headed out the door.

*****

Scott resisted everything she asked him these days. Most of the time she could deal with it, but when it came to parenting, she found it so difficult to let it go—especially as the bulk of the caregiving and parenting fell on her. Scott had no respect for her methods or ideas.

Noah had two decidedly different parents. They were never on the same page with anything. Geez, they weren't even in the same book! Food, mealtimes, bedtime, chores, showers, homework.

When Noah was younger, it used to be funny to her. She would joke, "Yes, I have two children. One is two, the other is thirty-eight."

Little did she realize then how unfunny it would turn out to be. Or how accurate her blithe comment was to become.

It wasn't just that he resisted, it was like he went out of his way to actually do the total opposite.

"Let's feed Noah less dairy foods." Scott would buy him cheese sticks and ice cream bars.

"Let's make sure Noah eats more fruit and veggies." Scott would buy him Lunchables and the highly colored processed TV meals in a box.

"Let's make sure Noah is only on his devices for an hour at a time." Scott would let him sit in the same spot on the couch all day when she was at work, playing on his iPad.

"Please don't buy Noah a toy or treat every single time we go to a store." Scott would buy Noah a treat or a toy every time they went to any store.

"Let's set up a system so Noah earns his pocket money." Scott would just give him money any time he asked.

"Let's keep Noah on a regular bedtime routine." Scott would regularly start movies for them to watch at 7:00 p.m.

"Let's make sure Noah is upstairs in his bedroom by X time, in bed by X time, and lights out by X time." Scott would see every night that he was home as some sort of special treat and didn't see the point of enforcing bedtime.

On and on it went. Gemma wouldn't be so pissed about it if Scott actually stepped in with another idea and followed it through, but he didn't. There was no question about how much Scott loved Noah, but it felt to Gemma like he was just there to blow any routine or discipline habits out of the water with no other solution or alternative—which in turn forced Gemma to be the enforcer parent. *"It's so unfair,"* she would grumble to herself, *"how come he gets to be the good-time Dad?"* Scott would say she should just go with the flow. She couldn't, she took her responsibility of teaching and shaping Noah into a functioning human so that he would be able to have the tools to navigate his own life very seriously. Scott did not.

*****

Gemma was nervous as she drove over to where the Al-Anon meetings were held. She felt like she had something stuck in her throat and kind of sick at the same time. She wondered if she might throw up.

As she pulled into the parking lot of the meeting hall, she could see people greeting each other, older women mainly, about five or six of them with books in hand, looking like they were going to a book study, chatting and laughing with each other. *Oh boy.* Gemma felt more intimidated than ever. Maybe it was the wrong place. She thought to herself she should just leave. She knew it wasn't the wrong venue though. She knew she had to go in but remained glued to her car seat, paralyzed with fear.

She sat and watched and waited until everyone had gone into the building, too terrified to move. *What if they laughed at her? What if they thought she was crazy and just being a drama queen? What if she was supposed to have registered somewhere or something first?*

Or worse, what if they just totally ignore her? She should probably just go home, sure she'd just be wasting everyone's time.

Good grief, woman! Just go! She pep-talked herself, took a deep breath, and got out of the car with shaking hands. She took another deep breath. Was she going to be sick? She walked on wooden legs toward the front door of the meeting place. Her feet didn't feel like her own, and she wondered if she was just going to fall over. It still wasn't too late. She could just go back to the car and go home, nobody had seen her.

As she stood at the door, still frozen with fear, a friendly "Hi there" sounded from behind her. Gemma whirled around like she'd been shot and was greeted by a tall, older lady with dancing blue eyes and a warm smile. "Are you coming in? It's a bit overwhelming your first time." She went on. "My name is Diane." She held the door. "What's yours?"

"Um, I'm Gemma," she replied, walking through the door. She paused inside the building, unsure of which door to head toward.

Diane walked past her. "That's a pretty name you don't hear much across the Atlantic. Is your family British?" Diane winked at her, again not giving her a chance to answer. "This way."

"How do you know where I'm going?" Gemma asked.

"Al-Anon, right? You look as terrified as I felt the first time I came to a meeting."

Gemma laughed, an awkward surprised laugh, in spite of herself. "Gee, I thought I had my cool, calm, and collected face on."

Diane winked at her again. "It'll be okay, you're safe here." *What a strange thing to say*, Gemma thought to herself. But at the same time, she found it comforting.

They were at the door now, and Diane went in first.

Everyone was sitting at a large round table. One lady was reading something from a folder. The ones that did turn toward her looked straight at her and smiled. One of them moved over and got up to pull a chair in for Gemma to sit on. Another one pushed a book over to the spot where she would be sitting and whispered, "There's coffee over there if you want some." She motioned to the corner of the room.

Gemma returned the smile, and mouthed back, "Thank you." She also smiled at the lady who had pulled over a chair and made space for her.

Diane was right. For the first time in so long, she couldn't even remember, Gemma felt comfortable and safe. She realized in that instant how she was continually on edge at home and around Scott.

It wasn't until later that Gemma realized there were no men at the meeting. She sat and cried for most of the time, relieved and validated just by listening to their meeting and the other women talking about the alcoholics they loved in their lives. The lady next to her that had offered her the coffee, just gave her a box of Kleenex and didn't ask her to share or anything. Diane moved over and sat next to her and patted her on the shoulder. After a while, she managed to pull herself together and apologized for wrecking their meeting. She was met with warm smiles. "You didn't wreck our meeting, dear. This is what we are here for. We have all been where you are." Gemma just sniveled and nodded gratefully. She listened to more women speaking and followed along with the meeting as best she could. She felt so much better to not feel so alone. This was an actual thing. She learnt something new, that effectively removed her blindfold concerning the situation she was in. Alcoholism isn't a choice, it's a disease. You didn't cause it, you can't control it, and you can't cure it.

And she also learnt a new way to verbally protect herself and validate her feelings when she was being made to feel guilty or incompetent: "I love you, but I love me more."

As she left, she was given several warm hugs and phone numbers and some pamphlets and a book. She felt better and stronger than she had in a long time, again realizing how awful she had been feeling for so long. It's funny how we get used to feeling bad constantly, but it's not until we start taking positive action in our lives that we fully realize how bad we really feel, Gemma pondered, as she promised herself to return next Thursday.

Gemma sat in her car and took several deep breaths before she headed home. Feeling grounded but also sad yet hopeful, she realized how bad it had really gotten. She also felt bad for Scott. And Noah.

As she drove home, she decided she would go to that church. It would be nice to feel like she was part of something, to belong somewhere. She would also like Noah to feel like he belonged somewhere too, not just with her. Without close family or any siblings and even without a strong male mentor, she really wanted him to have some positive influences.

It seemed Scott had decided his place to belong was definitely not at home with his family or even with her anymore. Overcome with futility again and feeling like a horrible mother, she cried the rest of the way home. She left all the info in the glove box in her car, doubting her own perceptions of the situation. Was he really that bad? Did she really need to go to Al-Anon? Even as she doubted herself, she knew it was the right thing for her to do. *Why do we always put ourselves last when we need help?* She pondered this question as she walked in the door. Scott was semiconscious on the couch. Noah was sitting in the corner of the couch on his device, still in his school uniform. The remains of Easy Mac was still sitting on the table, complete with spoon still in it.

"Mommy!" Noah jumped up and ran over for a big hug. Scott sat up, acting as if he had been alert the whole time.

"Didn't get a chance to get Noah in the shower, huh?" Gemma asked him.

"It's still early, what's the big deal?" Scott replied.

"The big deal is that it's eight fifteen, and Noah is not clean or in bed. I only asked you to do one thing, Scott." She let out a disappointed sigh. She couldn't be bothered waiting for a reply. It was obvious he was buzzed, and she didn't feel like having a fight either.

Gemma guided Noah down the hall toward his bedroom. She turned the shower on and checked the temperature for him. Noah loved for her to sit on the toilet seat and chat while he was in the shower. He would tell her all about his day and every other thing he was thinking of. Gemma cherished these moments, ten or so minutes to just sit in the steamy bathroom and chat with her boy. She loved hearing about his ideas and plans. She knew this phase would be over way too soon. They talked about going and checking out the community church and that it had a band and a children's ministry and would be different to anywhere else they had been, but she thought they would both like it. Noah agreed.

Chapter 9

Worship and All Things Church

Gemma checked with Pamela, who had originally told her about the community church. She even looked it up online to check directions and service times, twice. She felt nervous—again.

When she reminded Noah about the church they had talked about, he was excited. That was all the encouragement she needed. The following Sunday, while Scott was still snoring (as he'd only gotten home a few hours before), they went to the community church.

Noah was so delighted to be going to a church with a band, it was all he talked about in the car on the way there. This was enough motivation to turn around and drive back down the drive after they missed it the first time. Previously in life, she would have just kept driving once she'd realized her mistake. They followed the signs and were directed to a parking spot by a friendly man in a high visibility vest holding a coffee cup. He had a big smile and seemed to look straight at her. She waved back. He called out such a big friendly "Hello! Welcome!" when they got out of the car, she couldn't help but wonder if he had mistaken them for someone else.

As they walked in the front doors, they were greeted by an older lady who also wore a big genuine smile. "Welcome!" she held out a program. "Is this your first time here?"

Gemma nodded.

"Well, we are happy you chose to worship with us. We have a coffee station just over there"—she motioned to the left—"and you can check your son in right over here." She motioned to an archway to the right. "My name is Chris. Welcome." She handed her a Bible and a leaflet.

Gemma felt slightly less nervous. She took a breath and put her hand on Noah's shoulder. "Alright, son, this way." She hoped he didn't pick up on her nerves, although he was probably used to it by now.

She got him checked in and to the kids area. Everyone was so nice and friendly and helpful, she was almost suspicious at how friendly they were. Again, she silently berated herself, people can just be genuinely happy and friendly! Why was she so suspicious of everyone these days? Geez.

She met the older man in charge of the second graders, and he warmly shook her hand and Noah's, "Welcome, son, come in and meet our disciples for the day." He winked at Gemma. "We've got some great craft activities for them today. It ties in with the current message series."

Gemma smiled as if she knew what "message series" meant and made her way back to the main area. There was a band singing worship songs she recognized from the radio station they had begun to listen to, and she found her way to a seat.

For the next forty minutes, she was completely mesmerized—the music, the energy, the pastor who spoke so well—and it felt like the sermon was written for her. The message series she discovered was "Who do you think you are?" Gemma was attentive, for the first time in ages distracted from her own problems and her own thoughts and heartache. It felt good to sing and sit in the dark and just listen. She even laughed a little. She was hooked. It felt like the pastor was talking directly to her. *How did he know?*

She knew though this was bigger than a coincidence. She knew she was meant to be here, experiencing this. She couldn't quite admit to herself that this was God at work in her life right now, guiding her. *So, why does it feel so hokey to admit that?*

She remembered all the "born again" Christians' enthusiasm from her college days which was weird and scary. The language they used and way they explained how Jesus and God had such fantastic effects on their lives was simultaneously off-putting and terrifying and also sounded rehearsed, like they were trying a little too hard to sell their brand of "salvation." This feeling and experience had really stuck with her throughout the years.

But for the first time in her life, she had a glimpse of what they were trying to explain, and it was pretty accurate. She still wasn't comfortable with that language though.

At the end of the service, Gemma collected Noah, and they headed home.

They were both in good spirits. Noah chatted all the way home about the fun things they had done with the children's ministry, how he had made some new friends, and couldn't wait to go back next week.

Gemma felt great, for the first time in ages, she felt peaceful with her life.

Maybe it wasn't the life she had expected, but she was not alone.

They continued going every Sunday morning. Gemma was happy it felt like they were getting into a good routine. She hadn't really made any friends or anything, but it was nice to be recognized and feel welcome somewhere. She was unsure how to actually make friends with someone at a church. People were pleasant but obviously in their nuclear family groups—Mom, Dad, and the kids, or husband and wife. There didn't seem to be anyone in the congregation who was there alone. Oh well, she needed this support anyway. It was a safe place to be relatively anonymous. Not having superficial people wanting to know everything suited her.

She also kept attending the Thursday night meetings when she could (which was actually only every second week or so, Scott's schedule was difficult to pin down during the week).

She liked being there more than the thought or the action of actually getting there.

The weeks she did not make it, she would question if she even needed to go. It wasn't like Scott was an actual full-blown alcoholic or anything.

It seemed when she did make it, the theme for that week was incredibly relevant in her life that week. She cried a few more times when there, but it felt good. Again, although these women were very nice to her and kept giving her their phone numbers and taking hers, she didn't feel like there were any lasting friendships being built. These women were retired and in completely different places in their lives. Most of them seemed to be attending these meetings on account of someone's drinking in their lives years or even decades ago. She was a little wary of this, as she did not want to end her story here. There was a lot more life she intended on living, and her story would not get converted into a permanent loop here! Besides, she would never have the courage to actually call any of them or even answer if one of them called her. She appreciated the safe space though and getting to share her story without explanation or apology was very cathartic.

It all helped. Gemma really had not realized how reclusive and withdrawn she had become, feeling as though somehow this was all her fault. She was feeling more peaceful in herself and her life—less alienated, more validated. More at ease with her place in the world right now. More herself. She could feel herself returning to herself from wherever it was that she had been while going through all this—whatever this was.

This in turn helped her view her marriage a little differently. She felt more relaxed at home. Sure, Scott was still staying out late and being unreliable with his word, but they were fighting less. Gemma just let so much more go because it really didn't seem like it mattered or would make any difference. She found herself turning more and more to God. When she was at work one day, Vera, one of the older ladies that worked in the jewelry department, randomly gave her a Daily Devotional. Gemma was surprised. She had never really talked about anything beyond everyday pleasantries with Vera, and she had never used a Daily Devotional before, nor had she wanted to. But she was touched by the gesture and opened it to that day's date. Immediately she was hooked. The words and reading for the day were so appropriate (again) that she had stopped being surprised at such coincidences.

She noticed she had more compassion for Scott. What if his excessive alcohol consumption was a real sickness? Could that be true? She still didn't know if she totally believed that train of thought, but she was open-minded. Deep down, she believed that drinking (and habitually getting wasted in whatever form) was just a form of escape. Someone didn't want to deal with something uncomfortable or awkward or painful, either in themselves or in their lives, so they escaped—any way they could. She believed this because she had observed this in herself and the people she used to hang with in her own party days. (And once she had made the observation, it really took the "magic" out of the drinking and partying for her. That, and the wasted day being sick and hungover. She didn't like that part at all. And even after the best nights, a small part of her felt ashamed she'd wasted so much time and money).

As disappointing as it was to admit, she knew Scott would always avoid having difficult or uncomfortable conversations with anyone about anything. He could talk to people, and he could argue a point, but setting personal boundaries and confronting someone he knew about their behavior would send him running. He would always rather turn on the charm and have someone else do it for him but in a way that would let them think it was their idea. He always wanted to be seen as the good guy.

They weren't any closer, but their fights seemed less intense. Gemma realized they were only fighting as it was the only way she was getting attention from him (and he from her?); she still got angry at his blatant opting out of any family obligations, but honestly, if he didn't want to be with them, he wasn't going to be, no matter how angry she got. That was that.

She was even less on guard about Janine calling and dropping by for whatever random reasons. Gemma noticed Janine was a very needy person, continually searching for validation or support or advice or whatever attention she could get for any trivial reason. It was very high school (still) to Gemma. There really was no other way to describe it...immature? Janine seemed friendly enough besides *that* obvious character flaw. *Who knows, that's probably attractive to some people.* She was pretty in that stereotypical blonde big busted way. There was nothing outstanding about her look. She looked like so many other girls in their early thirties, a legend in her own lunchtime. Gemma wasn't particularly threatened by her. Janine liked to wear those active wear leggings with the cutouts when she wasn't at work (although honestly Gemma did not know what she looked like at work), and her legs did kind of look like they were stuck on to her body at strange angles. Her makeup always looked like she had taught herself from a Kardashian tutorial video on YouTube but skipped the bit on the importance of blending. Gemma tried not to judge other people's makeup skills, but sometimes she just could not help but make the observation. She didn't even know if Janine knew Gemma was a makeup artist. Gemma couldn't be bothered telling her either. It's not like Janine ever was interested in anyone else but herself anyway.

Chapter 10

Earthquakes

Some things remained unchanged, however. Scott was still staying out till all hours and coming home stinky and waking Gemma up, or she would wake up because he was not there and would text him and worry, then she would stay awake and lie in the dark till her alarm went off. She was actually getting used to having broken sleep, even more so than when Noah was a baby. Apparently five broken hours a night was her new normal. Sometimes when she fell asleep in Noah's bed, she would just stay there. At least that sleep was broken because Noah would kick or wiggle around at night or Gary would add himself to the bed. She would still listen for Scott, just to know he was home and safe.

Scott still always had some ridiculous lame excuse. Gemma went back and forth between being hurt, resentful, and dejected, or some days just completely detached. The mornings when he was passed out on the couch completely dressed (including his shoes), she would wake him up before Noah got up. She didn't want him to see his dad that way. She was disappointed that he did not want to be with her, occasionally she would still feel angry, but she was aware of an intense sadness, deep, deep inside her. Was she grieving? She knew he did not want to be with her anymore, no matter what his words said. Sometimes he still reached for her in his sleep, and she would snuggle into his warmth and familiarity. Their bodies still fit side by side wrapped around each other. Those nights she would fall into a restless light sleep, listening to his fitful breathing, missing the beautiful nights she had known with him for so long, where sleep came easily and was restful and refreshing. She had been a loved woman, and that quiet confidence carried her day after day for years. Now she was alone—emotionally deserted and mentally abandoned, while he was right in front of her. Having him continually out and drinking or home and hungover was almost worse than actually physically being alone. She often wondered where the whole theory of God using her as a frying pan fitted in this situation, and her life in general at the moment. Was she just on a low simmer for all those years? Gently bubbling away, mellowing, developing depth and richness, blending into a wonderful symphony of…what? Her illusion of a shared future?

Then Scott would do a total one hundred-eighty-degree turn and make an effort to make them dinner or clean the bathroom or put away the laundry and seem to listen when they'd be home together. This would give Gemma a renewed hope that he still loved her, and he still cared about her. But it wasn't the same attention he had given her before. This attention was diluted, distracted. When she was alone with her thoughts (which was often), and dissecting every interaction, she did not know where she stood with him anymore, even when he did listen, or acted like he was listening, it felt so empty and one-sided, he never offered any of his own thoughts or opinions. Gemma put it down to him being so busy with work and was appreciative of his attention, however limited, although all in all, his mixed messages were draining at best. She felt off balance around him. Gemma started getting up an hour earlier than usual so she could pray and go for a run, some time to herself so that she felt she had some control somewhere in her life.

One Sunday as winter was beginning to loosen its grip on their beach town, Gemma and Noah woke up early and decided to go to the earlier service at church. Scott had only been home for a few hours. Gemma had heard him come in and come to bed in the wee small hours.

Gemma and Noah were fairly used to being on their own in the mornings. Scott seldom got up to hang out or take Noah to school anymore, so this Sunday was no different to any other day really. They left the house and went to church. Gemma actually saw a couple whose son had been in Cub Scouts with Noah, and they had greeted her like an old friend. Gemma was surprised at how nice that made her feel. Noah had a great time with their son in the kids ministry that day too. They all stood around and chatted after church and made plans to try and get together soon.

They headed back to their car as the people were parking and heading in for the next service. The sun was shining, and Gemma felt closer to normal than she had for a long time. It felt good.

When they got back to the car, she checked her phone and saw a missed call from Scott, from thirty minutes beforehand. In the car, she tried calling him back, but he didn't answer. *Oh well*, she thought to herself, *can't have been that important. We'll be home in a few minutes anyway.*

When they got home, Scott was up, sitting on the couch reading something on his phone and drinking coffee. He looked terrible. Probably hungover, Gemma automatically assumed.

"Hi, honey." She kissed his head. "You look rough. Did you have a hard night?"

She almost expected an immediate snap back in reply. He didn't say anything. He didn't have the usual sat-in-a-bar-drank-and-smoked-for-hours smell. She remembered she had noticed that last night as he got into bed.

Scott gave her a weary look. "You have no idea." He gave a big sigh without looking back down to his phone.

Gemma felt a wave of compassion sweep over her. "Try me." She smiled. "Are you hungry? Do you want some eggs?"

Scott nodded and told her about the drama he had to deal with the night before; a couple had gotten into a fight at the bar, and the woman threw her drink on the man but got most of it on another female customer next to him. She was pissed and started yelling too. Her partner stepped up to the guy in the original fight, and the two men started yelling and shoving each other, heading quickly for an all-out brawl. The original couple were so drunk, they kept arguing and hurling abuse at each other, as well as trying to take on everyone else.

Scott, Mark, and Ryan had to enlist the help of one of the bigger waiters to escort the couple out of the restaurant. To add to the chaos, one of the other wait staff had slipped and fallen as he came back into the kitchen, knocked himself out, and ended up with stitches and a concussion, then the man from the argument at the bar pulled a gun on a good Samaritan in the parking lot who had tried to step in and stop them fighting in the parking lot. Within thirty minutes, Scott ended up having to call an ambulance and the police—for the first time in his GM career, both on the same night. And deal with the aftermath; contacting the restaurant owners, giving police statements, contacting the Marshside Mama's lawyer, as well as finishing up one of the busiest nights yet, one waiter down.

Gemma listened as she cooked him some breakfast and made a fresh pot of coffee. She felt bad for him. It really did sound like a terrible never-ending night.

As he ate, they talked about what he had to do now concerning both situations and how crazy it had all been. It wasn't even full moon!

They drank coffee together, and it felt like old times, just being there for each other, talking, like friends—figuring it out.

When Scott got the call from Rob McKay to meet him in an hour to discuss the events of the night before, even he seemed disappointed that his work day was starting earlier, and their conversation was over so soon. They shared a long hug and a slow soft kiss before he left. He cupped her face in his hands and thanked her for being there. "Always," she replied.

He called her three times that night from work to let her know what was up and how things were going. She made him dinner so he had something to eat when he got home (something she stopped doing months ago, as he never ate it), and when he called to say goodnight to Noah (which he had also not done in months), he asked when her next day off was and suggested they spend the day together, maybe go out and have breakfast together after getting Noah off to school and play a few holes of golf or something. He said it felt like too long since they had spent any meaningful time together. She agreed and felt hopeful and even a little excited, getting to hang with Scott all to herself, some one-on-one time. She had really missed that with him. They had previously spent so much time together. It was hard just not having any these days.

The next couple of days felt like "normal" to her (what she remembered normal as being, whatever that was). Scott was home early (well, not long after the restaurant closed) and would shower before bed. His drinking was minimal, and it was nice to have him next to her—present, loving, and sweet, affectionate, hilarious Scott. They even made love a couple of times. Lulled into a false sense of security by this sudden return to normal, Gemma squashed any feelings of doubt and started to relax a little. Everything was settling back to normal. He was keeping his word to Noah and spending time with him too, which Gemma felt most happy about.

She wondered if her new feelings of validation and peace had anything to do with it.

Does how you feel inside reflect what happens outside? She knew she had read plenty of spiritual wisdom that pointed out exactly this fact. Wasn't it even mentioned in the Bible? Gemma had never really understood exactly how it translated to everyday life. She often thought she did, but this week it took on a deeper meaning.

The next day off they had together was the following Thursday. They planned to hang out as Scott had suggested. On Wednesday, he was working the day shift, so Gemma said she'd cook one of his favorite meals for them and have dinner ready when he got home.

He wasn't sure exactly of the time, he thought around five would be a safe bet. When he called her just after she got home with Noah, he thought maybe a little after 5:00 p.m. He had to wait on his assistant manager to finish the kitchen inventory with Sooz, and he would bring a bottle of their favorite pinot noir with him.

Gemma didn't really think much of it when he still wasn't home by 5:20 p.m. At 5:45 p.m., he texted her to say something had come up. He was running late and would be home soon.

At 6:15 p.m., Gemma was feeling a little irritated that he didn't answer her texts, and that her call went to voicemail. She decided to feed Noah and sat down with him while he ate. He kept asking where Dad was and why he wasn't home by now because he said he would be home. Gemma said she didn't know. Although she could feel herself getting more and more upset every time he asked, she reminded herself it wasn't Noah's fault, but still, her temper was becoming increasingly shorter.

After dinner, she hung out with him for a little while going over his reading homework but feeling herself losing her grip on the peaceful loving feelings she'd had for the last few days. Dinner was looking sad and dry. Gemma was hungry. Should she just go ahead and eat? But she had been looking forward to hanging out and eating with Scott. She felt such a mixture of emotions—upset and rejected, like she'd been stood up, but disappointed predominantly.

Why won't he answer my texts? Or my calls? Where is he? Is he okay? Is everything okay at work? Should I call the restaurant? Is he drinking somewhere?

At 7:00 p.m., she told Noah it was time to get organized for bath and bed. He again asked where his Dad was.

"I don't know!" Gemma snapped. "It's time for your bath anyway."

Noah looked slightly offended but bounced back instantly. Gemma felt a pang of guilt.

"Can we call him?" he asked hopefully.

"Sure." Gemma sighed, suddenly feeling emotional, deflated, and stupid. She waited for it to start ringing and handed the phone to Noah.

She heard Scott answer and could tell from where she was standing that he was drunk in a bar. He sounded irritated when he answered, expecting it to be her no doubt, she thought to herself. She heard his voice soften once he realized it was Noah.

"When are you coming home, Dad? Will you be here in time to tuck me in?" he asked. His innocence killed her. *He probably won't be home till much later*, she thought bitterly.

She went to the kitchen and turned off the oven. She pulled out her own dinner. She felt even more deflated. Like if she didn't have to keep standing up and looking after Noah, she would be a puddle of self-pity on the floor——spineless and jelly-like. She totally should have seen this coming a mile away.

Hanging out with other people and alcohol wins again.

She didn't know whether she was jealous or angry.

She could hear Noah talking, well, answering. "Uh-huh. Yes, Dad. Okay, yes, I will," etc. Then he came in to the kitchen and handed her the phone. He headed down the hall towards his room.

"Hi, honey." She tried to make herself sound happy to hear from him. "What's up? Your dinners going to be—" she asked lightly, but Scott interrupted her.

"Why did you make Noah call me?" he hissed at her.

"What?" Gemma took a step back like she'd been hit. Her throat tightened, and she felt hot. "What are you talking about?"

"You know exactly what I'm talking about, using Noah to manipulate me and make me feel guilty!" he slurred slightly.

"Excuse me?" Gemma felt a rush of anger. "Your son misses you and wants to talk to you! How dare you accuse me of using him to make you feel anything! *You said you'd be home two hours ago!*" She yelled the last sentence.

"I ran into one of our beer reps who just got engaged and am just having a beer before I head home. I didn't think it would be a big deal! Since when am I supposed to ask *you* for permission to have a dam beer?" he retorted. She felt like he was saying that crap to look like the big man in front of whoever the hell he was with, which pissed her off even more.

"Well, when your wife is waiting on you to eat dinner with you and you don't answer your texts or phone calls and you're two hours late. *It is* a big deal!" she snapped back. "What the hell, Scott?" she went on. "Doesn't our dinner or day off together mean anything to you? What happened to dinner and a bottle of wine? I'm waiting for you to eat here!"

There was a long pause. She couldn't tell if he was actually processing what she'd just said or if he had his hand over the phone and was talking to someone else.

"I'm sorry, I'll be home soon."

He didn't sound sorry, and she knew he would not be home soon. She wasn't even sure if he knew the meaning of what he'd said or if he was just saying it to calm her down.

Gemma hung up without saying anything. That was the least sincere sounding apology she'd heard in a while.

She got Noah in the bath, promising him she'd be back as soon as she had something to eat.

Her dinner was not as great as it would have tasted two hours ago, but she ate it anyway, having a momentary pang of guilt that Scott's was now sitting in a cooling oven.

She was angry at herself, and at him, for once again letting herself be suckered in by his stupid lies and by the obvious fact he wasn't really as excited to be spending time with her as she thought he was or she was with him.

This thought made her feel like someone had punched her in the stomach.

Gemma put her head in her hands and started crying. She felt hopeless and lost.

What was he doing? What was she doing? She had really thought everything was going to return to normal.

Why?

Because he was relatively sober for three days? And she just wanted him to be? That was the stupidest thing ever. What was codependent? Is this something she could influence? This was her life too. Why couldn't she just leave? Where would she go? This thought made her feel even more lost and lonely. What had she let herself become?

Scott got home shortly after midnight. Gemma was awake. Her eyes felt hot and puffy from crying off and on for hours. She had the window open and was sitting on the windowsill. The cold breeze felt good on her hot face. She wished she had someone to talk to. She had thought about calling her sister, but they hardly spoke at all, and she really couldn't bring herself to admit she didn't know what to do. Leave? Stay? Scott had a problem, there was no doubt about that. She had tried to pray, with a little success. She felt herself get calm and still for a moment but then would be overcome with emotion again. She didn't even know if she was doing it right.

When she heard him come in, she got in bed, feeling for a moment like she'd just been caught doing something wrong. She lay in the dark, feeling alone and hopeless, although her curiosity piqued as she could hear Scott as usual in the kitchen stumbling around, but he was talking. To himself? No, it was actually to someone? Was he on the phone? What on earth? She heard him end the conversation and come down the hall. He came into the nearly dark room sat on the bed. He put his hand on her leg. "Are you awake?" He sounded concerned.

"Yes," she answered.

"Gem, I'm sorry." He sounded choked up. "I thought I could just go for one beer. I couldn't stop drinking. I just wanted to keep going. I couldn't say no. I don't know what to do, Gem. I'm just a loser." Gemma sat up and turned the bedside lamp on, staring at him. Was he serious? She couldn't tell if he was having a genuine moment of self-realization and remorse or if he was totally playing her.

"You're not a loser, Scott." She took his hand. "I think you have a problem with alcohol, that's it. There's no need to get all judge-y on yourself. Do you think you have a problem? Does that happen every time you go out drinking?"

He looked at her blankly with bloodshot eyes, like he had no idea what she was talking about. "All I said was that I couldn't stop drinking tonight. I didn't mean that happened all the time."

Gemma was caught off guard by his defensiveness. Didn't he just ask for help? WTF? She changed the subject, dancing around the elephant in the room. "Who was on the phone?' she asked him.

He looked confused. "What do you mean?"

"Just now, I heard you on the phone," she pressed.

"Oh, Janine was calling to make sure I got home okay," he replied.

Gemma felt a rush of jealousy. He was out with her? "I thought you said you were with the beer rep." Gemma tried to keep her tone light but was working hard to not just lose her temper and her mind. She knew he was wasted and knew they would just have a big stupid pointless fight. She took a deep trembling breath in, comprehending the situation. So he totally blew off a night with her and Noah to go out drinking with his work buddies, not just buddies but younger, hotter chicks? What was that? A better offer?

Scott let out a big sigh and lay back with his eyes closed. "Janine and Kelly were first cut so they joined us, then Nick came later too. I didn't realize it would be a big deal." He sounded defensive again.

Gemma was pissed. "I don't get it, you said you'd be home for dinner, that we'd hang out and you were bringing wine. Do you remember that part? Do you remember that you said you were looking forward to it? That you would be home straight after work? Then two hours later, you said you would be home soon. That was five hours ago Scott! Five *hours*!" frustrated and feeling completely worthless, Gemma started crying again in spite of herself. She felt dizzy. What the hell was this? Was he playing games with her?

"I didn't promise anything." Scott kept his eyes closed. "Look, I'm really tired. I'll sleep on the couch if you want."

"That's a good idea." Gemma turned off the light and lay down.

Scott didn't move. Within a few minutes, he started snoring. She fantasied about him dying in his sleep, then it would all be over, and she wouldn't have to deal with any of this mess. It would be a whole new mess she would be dealing with. Wow, no matter which way she looked at it, she was in deep, and it was going to take a lot of time and heartache to get out.

She was aware that she was in the middle of a giant spiderweb. There was no easy way out of this one. She felt bad wishing his death but acknowledged it was just a thought from a tired emotional mind and let it go. Gemma lay there for what seemed like forever, staring at the ceiling. Eventually she got up and took his shoes off. She hated it when he fell asleep with his clothes on. It was even worse when he left his shoes on!

She went into the kitchen and got herself a glass of water. 3:12 a.m. The clock on the stove pointing out how late it was, and how unexpectedly shitty her night had turned out. One of the things she hated most (who was she kidding, the whole situation sucked) was that she could always tell how drunk he was by how many lights he left on. Most nights she felt like the house was a glowing beacon in the neighborhood, boldly advertising that a drunk lived here, or worse, someone who never came home. It was so messed up because on the odd occasion she was ever out late, Scott never left a light on for her.

She turned off the lights and sat at the table in the dark. She had never been afraid of the dark; it had always been comforting to her, welcoming even. She took a deep breath in and started to pray.

"God, if you're there, I need help. Please guide me and give me the strength to know what to do for my family. Give me the strength to get through this. Give me the courage to keep going. Please help me."

She put her head down on the table and fell asleep.

Gemma woke up stiff and sore as the sky was becoming light. Gary was on the table licking her shoulder and cheek, pushing his head into hers, impatiently meowing and purring. Gemma sat up and stretched her neck, rolled her shoulders and let the memory of everything flood back in.

She let out a big long woeful sigh and wished it had all just been a crappy dream.

Wow, *that* wasn't how she'd envisioned her night turning out.

Gary kept nudging her; his solid warm head persistent and calming, keeping her focused on the morning in front of her.

"All right, buddy." She rubbed him under the chin and pressed her forehead into his, his deep purr vibrating in her brain.

Gemma got up from the table and got his food out of the fridge. She turned on the kettle to make herself some tea and put Gary's food down on his mat by the back door.

She heard herself sigh again, feeling downtrodden and angry that she was letting this happen to her. What was happening here? Honestly, if a friend was telling her the same story about what was happening in her marriage, she'd tell her to *run* and kick his drunk ass to the curb! That would have been from the perspective of a secure woman who had no clue how it felt to be in this position.

Although now she had a different perspective, a slim insight into why women stay.

Sure, she wasn't being physically abused in any way and wasn't concerned for her (or Noah's) safety or wellbeing (mainly, but she wondered more and more, exactly what was the true meaning of wellbeing?), but she kept returning to the thought; if one of her friends was in this situation, she would strongly encourage them to leave or make the guy leave. But how could she? What would she do? She knew nobody, had nobody here. She felt trapped. And scared. She still could not imagine or even envision herself separate from Scott. Their lives were seemingly, irrevocably intertwined. Just thinking about how or where to start the process was so overwhelming. She couldn't bring herself to give up hope just yet. Scott may be able to get his drinking under control. He had before. She knew it was possible. She knew the Scott she fell in love with and had so much history and good memories with must still be in there, somewhere. But where was he? How could she reach him?

She realized the full implication of investing your entire life in one person, especially when that one person has apparently had a change of heart or mind or succumbed to addiction. She should have seen this coming! She had seen it coming but had believed him when he said he always had everything under control. Why wouldn't she believe him? He had never given her any reason to doubt his word.

She felt utterly alone. There was no one she could talk to about this. She didn't want to go to a Women's Refuge or anything. Good grief! It wasn't *that* bad. Scott was destroying himself. Gemma was pretty sure he was completely oblivious to the fact that he was destroying his family in the process. What was so terrible in his life or memory that he was constantly trying to escape from? She pondered this question for a moment, staring out the kitchen window. The sky was the color of concrete, except for the slim space near the horizon that looked like the sun was burning orange trying to get through.

Gemma decided that she'd let Scott sleep. She didn't know what to say to him that she hadn't said before. She would take herself out for breakfast and do something for herself today—spend some quality time with herself. She needed some head space and could do with the break. Tonight she would take herself back to the Al-Anon meeting as well.

This decision was fueled by the fact he didn't even stir when she went into the room to get changed and use the bathroom to freshen up for the day. He was passed out, his heavy breathing on the verge of snoring. Screw him. She was perfectly capable of planning her own great day—by herself. So why did she feel so awful? Hollow and sick.

She shut the bedroom door and went down the hall and woke Noah up.

"Come on, buddy." She gently shook his shoulder. "Time to get up." Noah took a deep breath in and curled onto his side. "Sweetheart." She kissed him gently on his forehead.

Noah half-opened his eyes. "Is Dad home yet? What time is it?" He sat up, rubbing his eyes.

"Yes, honey, he's here. It's time to get up for school."

"Is Dad going to take me to school today?" Noah asked hopefully.

"I don't know." Gemma laid Noah's clothes out on the end of the bed for him. "Here you go, honey," she said, motioning to his clothes.

"Where's my hug?" he asked, stretching his arms out to her.

Gemma sat down on the bed next to him and wrapped her arms around his small frame. He hugged her tightly back. "I love you, Mom. Let's just stay here and hug."

"That would be great, wouldn't it?" Gemma asked him, imagining being able to just lay down right now and hug her little guy for the rest of the day. Such a delicious thought. Why shouldn't she just do that? Why did she feel so obligated to get him up and get him off to school on time with a full tummy? *Well, duh,* she told herself, *because that's what is supposed to happen. As his mom, it's my responsibility to instill in my small human a sense of purpose and responsibility, the importance of just showing up.* And because it just has to happen, she'd never really thought of school or work as something to be questioned or compromised. Such deep thoughts for such a weary mind.

They sat there for a few more moments, then Gemma snapped herself out of it. "Come on, let's get moving. How about this for a plan? I will start your breakfast, and maybe when you've got your clothes on, you can go see if Dad wants to wake up and take you to school."

Noah nodded and started to get out of bed. Gemma went back down the hall and started breakfast. Noah joined her a few moments later.

"Did he wake up?" she asked him, handing him a glass of water.

Noah shook his head. "He said, 'Five more minutes, I'm just collecting my thoughts' and rolled back over. He's probably not getting up, and he smells." Gemma was amused at Noah's impersonation of his dad's five-minute request and that "he smells" observation. Scott had used the "five more minutes" thing forever. At first, it was cute and then tedious. Now it was just predictable. Even Noah at eight years old was over it.

It was no surprise to either of them that Scott did not get up to join them in the rest of the time they were at home. Noah went in twice more to wake him up. Usually, Gemma would go in two or three times herself and entice him to alertness with a fresh cup of coffee, but today that was not happening. She couldn't even bring herself to turn the coffee maker on. Gemma gave Noah a big hug before they got in the car. "I'm sorry, Noah." She brushed his hair out of his face, struggling to find something to say…what? What could she say? *Sorry, your dad's a drunk? Sorry, he doesn't think we're important enough to keep his word to? Sorry, he has shitty values?*

"You know, almost everyone thinks I don't have a dad," he observed. "I thought he was different this week, that he would be like other dads, but he's still just the same." Noah stated it, simple as that.

He couldn't have said it better. She felt a pang of grief. *Out of the mouths of babes.*

"I know sweetheart, me too." She kissed his head. *Me too, son.*

Gemma was conscious to keep their conversation light and happy on the way to school. She didn't want him going into school feeling heavy and sad. It would be a crappy way for him to start his day. In the car rider line Noah remembered that his class was making a baking soda volcano for science and got excited, seemingly forgetting the disappointing start to the day, he leapt out of the car with a big smile. Gemma was relieved. Although heavy and sad was exactly how she felt. Rejected and neglected and awful. And in pain. She didn't know where exactly she hurt. She just hurt. Inside, outside, her head, her heart.

And confused. What was happening? To Scott? To her? To their marriage? It was increasingly obvious that they were on different trajectories in life. How could she bring them back in line? She had spent so long thinking she had her human, her man, forever and ever and ever. The thought that they may not be together forever had not really seemed like a possibility or even entered her mind. Was it still a possibility? Would their marriage make it through this?

Gemma shook that thought from her head. Her breath caught in her throat. *Was he having an affair?*

He never asked her to hang out anymore. She always used to be included in his work groups. Everyone always knew that he was married. Was he ashamed of her? Of Noah? Was he thinking about having an affair?

Gemma realized she was on a downward spiral with her thoughts. Not wanting to feel any worse, she pulled into the drive-through coffee spot and ordered herself a coffee, then she drove down to the beach and took off her shoes and socks. The sky was still an even grey and gloomy color, with no defined clouds or anything, just one equal covering of cloud blending seamlessly into the sea at the horizon. There was no one on the beach except way off in the distance. She could see a person on the shore and a dog running in the shallows. The sand felt cold between her toes, the hot coffee was stark contrast. She walked down to the water and stepped into the shallows. The small waves lapped at her feet, and the sudden cold took her breath away. It felt good though. The sea was still and grey with barely a swell. It looked heavy and dark and reflected her mood perfectly. Although this wasn't just "a mood," she didn't think she'd ever actually felt like this before.

Ironic, she pondered to herself, *I should have known the man who could build me up and make me feel invincible could also make me feel just as much in the opposite direction.*

Lord, what am I going to do? What is happening here? She looked up at the sky as if she expected him to just answer from the clouds.

Instead, all she saw was a lone seagull flying across the sky. Gemma took a slow walk along the sand, weighing her options. That didn't take long, she felt her options were limited. She couldn't imagine herself without Scott. She just couldn't. She couldn't imagine herself with anyone else, and she couldn't see herself alone. It was only ever him. Everything was just so normal and natural with him, she doubted she would ever find that with anyone else. Ever. Nor would she want to. He had a problem, and he needed her! Didn't he? She was pretty sure she still needed him. Didn't she?

The realization that she'd built her entire world around one person with the presumption that he felt the same way, when in actuality it appeared he did not, was enough to make her feel nauseous. This was potentially the biggest mistake she had ever made. Ever. She took a couple of deep breaths to calm the rising panic she felt.

She felt her phone vibrating in her jacket pocket. She couldn't even bring herself to pull it out. She knew it would be Scott.

Of course, as soon as she was overcome with the feeling of wanting to hear his voice, it stopped ringing.

She left the phone in her pocket. She didn't feel like hearing anything he had to say or trusted herself saying anything to him right now.

After she walked a little longer and her toes were red and cold, she realized how hungry she was and headed back to the car. Scott tried calling her twice more. She just looked at her phone but didn't answer. He sent her a "Where are you? I'm worried" text message.

She decided to text him back: "Out for breakfast, I'm fine."

"Call me," he replied.

Gemma ignored the request and brushed the sand off her feet. She put her socks and shoes back on. Where was she going to go for breakfast? It was 8:30 a.m. She remembered there was a twenty-four-hour diner not far from where she was, and it had always piqued her curiosity. The girls at work had often mentioned how good it was despite appearances. Gemma didn't care, she loved a good dive bar or rough-looking place. The more character the better, as far as she was concerned. She hated pretentious places where people went to see and be seen. Yes, she'd spent her fair share of time in them as well but would always be the first to suggest somewhere else.

She sat in the parking lot for a few minutes, contemplating whether or not to call Scott back. Eventually Gemma thought it best to just call because then she could eat in peace.

And she was raised to not play games. She hated them and didn't see the point.

If you had so little respect for someone that you lied to them and messed with their heads, why bother with them at all?

Ultimately, she still believed that one man and one woman should form an unbreakable bond, built on mutual unconditional love and respect, growing stronger and more productive over time through the years. Gemma realized she thought that's what she had, and she thought Scott was secure in that knowledge/belief too. Again, the thought hit her that it might not be true anymore. *Was it?* Again, Gemma felt nausea sweep over her, she took a deep breath.

She still wanted it to be true, so very much. She still loved him so much.

She just wanted it to go back to "them."

"Hey, where are you?" Gemma felt slightly smug that he sounded worried.

"Just getting something to eat," she replied.

"I thought we were going together?" he questioned.

"And I thought you were keeping your word and were coming home for dinner and to hang out with your family last night?" she questioned back.

"I told you when I came home. I had to have a drink with the beer rep after work."

"Um, *no*," Gemma called him out. "That's not what you said, and if you wanted to make me feel any less important to you, you pretty well covered it."

"Don't be like that. I've known him for ages, and he just got engaged. I hardly see him anymore," he offered.

"Don't be like what, Scott?" She could hear her voice becoming higher pitched. "You lied to me and Noah and totally blew us off, in favor of drinking with your stupid beer rep friend and your floozy waitresses from work for SEVEN HOURS?? I cooked dinner for us and waited and waited to eat with you, and when Noah called you because he was worried, you gave me a hard time because you thought I put him up to it!" Gemma said aggressively, she paused and took a deep breath. "How am I not supposed to be like anything except hurt and pissed off?"

There was a long silence, she heard him take a drag of cigarette. "You're right I'm just a piece of shit," he replied.

"No, Scott, I'm not accepting that either, cause then you don't think you have to do anything, just carry on with your lying and crappy behavior."

He was silent again.

"Hello?" Gemma asked. She went on, "Look, I'm hungry, and I need something to eat. We can talk later."

"When will you be home?" he asked.

"I don't know," she answered. "After I eat, I guess." She had no intention of going straight home after getting something to eat. Let him see how it feels when someone you love doesn't keep their word.

"I'm hungry too," he ventured. "Can I join you? Please? I'd still like to spend the day with you." He added hopefully. "I miss your beautiful face."

Gemma let out a big sigh (bastard). She did not want to have him use his charm on her. She was always a sucker for sweet talk. And she did miss him.

"If you have to."

She told him where she was, and he was there in a few minutes. They shared an uncomfortable hug. He smelt like alcohol and cigarettes.

"Couldn't you at least have had a shower or something?" she asked.

Scott shrugged. "I wanted to see you," he offered with a sheepish grin.

They sat down and ordered coffee. She felt surreal, like she couldn't believe they were just acting normally. She felt like her whole world was collapsing in on her, like she couldn't breathe properly. She wondered if this was what it felt like to have asthma, like she couldn't take a deep enough breath in.

They made random small talk about the menu. Scott said he'd never been there before either. Gemma didn't know whether to believe him or not. The waitress came and took their order.

And then it was just them—sitting there, looking at each other.

Gemma asked him what happened to his wedding ring. He said it was squashed between two kegs when he was changing them one night, and he had to take it off, but he was going to get it reshaped and put it back on. She pointed out that, that must have happened a few months ago because she remembered it not being on his finger the night they went to Janine and Daniel's cookout. Scott did his best "Really? I don't think so" look. Gemma returned his look with a "You know that's true" stare.

"Scott," she asked, "are you having an affair?"

He stopped and gave her a curious look. "No, Gemma, why would you think that?" he replied. He looked amused rather than busted. Gemma believed him. There was nothing in his expression to make her believe otherwise, not a single flicker in his eyes or flinch. *Still, the only affair is with alcohol*, she thought to herself.

She didn't say anything for a while. Scott asked if she was okay.

"Why would I not believe that? You're out all hours of the night, you have endless time for everyone else except the people that really love and need you, you're defensive as hell about everything, you have other chicks calling you late night. This is total BS." She searched his face for some reaction, some recognition that his behavior was creating so much havoc in their family life. She saw nothing.

She sighed. "I can't do this, Scott."

"Do what?" he asked.

"Whatever this is," she replied, "our lives, our relationship, our marriage, our family, I'm under the impression you hate all of it, and we are cramping your style. There are a dozen other things you'd always rather be doing or people you'd rather be with than us, and it sucks. You're killing me. I can't sleep when you're not home, and when you are home, I don't sleep because you smell and snore loud enough to rattle the windows."

She felt the tears welling up. "If you don't want to be with me, just say so."

He reached for her hand. "Gemma, we're just different people these days. You don't like anything I like. Other people are fine with relationships like ours."

She gave him an incredulous look. "We have never been *other people*, Scott!"

Right then, the waitress arrived with their breakfast, oblivious to her interruption. She made mundane small talk about how good the eggs benedict was today and what a great choice it was and if they needed more coffee and she could bring a pot.

"No, thank you," Scott cut her off. She looked at him and then Gemma, who was wiping her eyes, realized she must have interrupted something, and beat a hasty retreat.

"I think you should sleep in the spare bedroom." Gemma sniffed and reached for the pepper. She didn't really know what she was going to do with said pepper. She didn't feel very hungry at all, it just seemed like something to do. She was surprised as he was to hear those words come out of her mouth.

"Why?" Scott asked.

"Seriously?" she answered. "I haven't had a complete night's sleep in months. My life is series of shitty naps. I can't do it anymore. I need my sleep, Scott."

"I don't get very much sleep either," he replied defensively.

"Yes, but you are doing that to yourself," she bounced back. "I don't have the luxury of hanging out late night, drinking with friends or whoever and coming home whenever the hell I want and either crashing fully dressed on the couch or just going straight to bed without brushing my teeth or even washing my hands. Holy crap, Scott, I've asked you over and over to have a little bit of respect and to at least brush your teeth and wash your hands before coming to bed! But you don't, you won't. You act like it's the ultimate sacrifice on your part to do anything that looks like consideration to anyone but yourself."

She looked down at her food.

"Well, why don't you go out and make all the money then? Why don't you find a decent-paying job cause your job pays shit, and I'll stay home and look after Noah and take care of everything? It's not like you even keep a very clean house. There's always clutter and junk everywhere. I can't even sit down to eat at the dining room table without having to move everything first. There's always shit all over the kitchen counter and the breakfast bar too, or do you just want me to do that too? You don't have to do anything, I'll just do it all." He stared at her defiantly.

What the hell just happened? Gemma felt attacked—because she was! She was concentrating to remain focused on the actual point—the request for him to move into the spare room so she can sleep at night—and not get sucked into what he had just thrown at her. Did he really think that she did nothing? What the? That her contribution to their home was the equivalent of zilch?

She put a fork full of food into her mouth and chewed. The food felt like cardboard in her mouth. She didn't know whether to fight back, or cry, or both.

"You know, Gemma," he continued, "it's so hard to live with you because you are always so negative about everything. You never want to do anything I like to do, you bitch and moan about my friends, and then you make out like you do everything all the time and I don't do anything at all." He kept eating as if he was talking about the weather. "Your job pays shit money. I don't know why you just don't get a job in an office or something that pays better."

She looked at him as if he had two heads. She forced herself to swallow the mouthful—and the hurt angry feelings. And the feeling like she'd just been blindsided. This didn't sound like Scott talking, who had he been talking to? Why was he saying this? She searched her memory for times she was negative to him about anything. It was hard to focus; her thoughts were spinning. WTF? Had she been negative without realizing? Through it all, she had one clear thought loud and sudden like a laser beam: *he's totally playing me to throw me off balance. Right now, he'll say anything so that he's not the bad guy and didn't do anything wrong.* She wasn't sure where that came from. A book she'd read about addiction? One of the podcasts she always listened to? God himself? She didn't know, but it felt right, and if nothing else, Gemma always trusted her gut feelings. She didn't say anything for a moment, she just looked at him.

"Well, all the more reason for you to move into the spare bedroom then."

She took another mouthful, suddenly defiant. Two can play this game.

But she hated they were even playing any game. This had never been the way they operated or related to each other. What was happening here?

"Fine," Scott snapped. "Thanks for ruining breakfast," he added.

"I ruined breakfast?" she snapped back. "Says the guy who stood up his wife and child in favor of drinks with a stupid beer rep and the staff from his work."

"At least they know how to have fun," he retorted.

Wow, of course Scott liked to hang out and drink and party with his staff. They all thought he was great. They respected what he said and thought he was cool. He didn't have to "show up" for any of them beyond being the head cool kid. Not like being a husband and Dad, where he was expected to add value and have substance as a decent human being.

Gemma was enraged but caught herself. He was just trying to engage her in some way, albeit negatively. She took a breath to regain composure.

"Wow, Scott, you can never admit when you are wrong, can you? Why can't you ever say, 'I messed up, I'm sorry'? Why do you think just attacking me will make you right? Remember I know you probably better than anyone else in your life."

He looked at her with…what, surprise? She was sure that's what she saw on his face, just a flicker, for just a moment. Did that mean she was right? Did she get in there somehow? That was actually the closest thing to a reaction she'd seen on his face for a long time. The more he drank, the less compassion and empathy he seemed to have anywhere for anything or anyone in his life.

"Okay, if that's what you want," he answered.

She presumed he was talking about the room thing. "It is," Gemma answered.

They finished their meals in stony silence.

Scott started sleeping in the spare room a few nights later. Gemma couldn't understand why it took him so long to do it.

He hadn't apologized to her for the night he stood them up. When Noah questioned him about it, he offered a "I'll make it up to you" without any specifics, which pissed Gemma off. Noah was still too young to realize that his dad was just saying anything to get out of an uncomfortable situation where he knew he had messed up. Scott didn't seem to notice that Noah still hung on his every word.

Knowing that Scott really didn't have any intention of following through but not wanting to be the one spoiling her son's hero worship for his dad, Gemma gave Noah a big hug when he asked her what surprise his dad would have for him to make it up to him. "I don't know, honey." She gave him another big hug. "I don't know." Gemma didn't see it as her place to destroy his opinion of Scott. As far as she could see, he was on track to do that just fine on his own.

Chapter 11

Time Marches On

Scott's behavior was a little more controlled over the next week or so. He seemed to have genuine remorse for how their marriage was failing but not enough to actually make an effort to repair anything or take responsibility for his actions or alter his behavior Gemma noted. Or apologize.

Looking back over the course of their relationship though, this was how it always had gone, no matter who was in the wrong, Scott would behave as if there had not really been a problem, and she would let it go, realizing that there was no point in holding a grudge—except nothing was ever resolved. Although until now, it had only ever been small stuff that she really didn't think was worth losing sleep over. Wasn't there a book written on just that? *Don't sweat the small stuff and it's all small stuff?* Wow. That realization was huge for her. Apparently she should have been sweating the small stuff, because now it had grown to be big stuff.

Gemma stepped up her efforts to attend Al-Anon more regularly. She found it gave her more peace and insight into her husband's behavior. There were still questions in her mind, and she really was not sure if he actually did "suffer from this illness." He was suddenly more interested in working out and his personal grooming (although he never had been a sloppy man, he had always taken pride in his appearance, but not in an overly self-absorbed way). He was almost vain all of a sudden.

One morning, Gemma returned to the horrible thought, *what if he really IS having an affair? Maybe that's what was happening, instead of him being on the slippery slope of alcoholism.*

Gemma always knew he had a bunch of female friends. She didn't mind. Being in makeup and film, she'd always had a bunch of male friends too, but previously their friendships were open and inclusive. Now it seemed that Scott was almost secretive with the girls he hung out with. Whenever Gemma asked who he was out with, he would be vague and elusive, with a dismissive, "just the usual crew from work."

Previously, if either one of them saw or thought that one of the other friends of the opposite sex was getting too friendly and they mentioned it to each other, they would respect each other's feelings and tone down the friendship out of respect for their relationship. This rule that had done them so well for years, seemed to fly out the window.

When she tried to talk to Scott about it, he just blew it off, told her she was being paranoid, and questioned when he would even be able to have time to start a relationship with anyone. He used his old "why would I want to eat a hamburger out, when I have steak at home?" with a wink. Gemma blushed in spite of herself, but still she noticed changes. Previously, each other's phones had been open to each other to use, or look for something. Now Scott was very guarded with his phone. He turned off all notifications and set the locked screen to black. He also changed his access code and wouldn't even tell Noah what it was. When she asked him about that, he said it was to protect it at work as he often left it in the office or behind the bar, and he didn't want his employees messing with it.

That made sense, but she would drive herself crazy in the middle of the night when she was awake, waiting to hear him come home, letting her thoughts run away with her.

She had faith though that the good man she married was still in there and what he told her was the truth, as he had always told her the truth. Surely after this amount of time, she could still trust his word. But still…

Once Gemma had all these thoughts in line, she would be quite concerned about his fidelity, although on one hand, she knew he was getting so drunk so regularly she wondered if he could even get a hard-on anymore. However, she also knew what women were like, especially in this area of the South. Any woman that saw a man being nice to them, joking with them, answering their calls and text messages automatically assumed there was something more. She wouldn't put it past Scott to be leading on whoever without even realizing it.

He was the original party starter—friendly, engaging, funny, could talk to anyone about anything, would have a drink with anyone who wanted one, any time of the day or night, mainly because he wanted a drink not because of whatever the poor bitch was telling herself. This train of thought worried Gemma though.

She had tried talking to Scott a few times about it, but he would either tell her she was being paranoid or get defensive and accuse her of being jealous that he had a good group of friends and she did not. Of course, this would throw her off and send her thoughts in another direction, questioning herself. However although this worked for a while, slowly it began to dawn on her as she would be mulling it over (usually in the wee small hours), that he was just manipulating the conversation and distracting her, that he never actually put her fears to rest.

She couldn't help but notice Janine was all up in their lives daily. She had started texting Gemma about random kid stuff all the time too (where did you buy this? How do you cope with that? Do you have a recipe for this? Can I borrow a cup of milk/sugar/an egg?) Gemma stuck to her previous thoughts of how needy this chick was. She was also calling and texting Scott a lot about anything and everything to do with work or the schedule or a coworker or whatever. She also had a talent for showing up unannounced needing things or inviting them over to eat. Gemma would sometimes feel put out that she didn't even seem to have a say in what they got to do as a family, but other times she would feel grateful to have another family as friends they could hang out with sometimes, even though quite often she wasn't really included in the conversation or they would seem to have all their own work jokes and go into depth about their work situations. Deciding to be grateful rather than suspicious, Gemma would join in where she could. She didn't want to seem standoffish or anything, but honestly their conversations bored her. Once again it felt as petty and small minded as it had in high school.

She often wondered if she had an appropriate view of the situation. When she asked Scott about Janine's constant contact, he seemed oblivious. She seemed to be the self-appointed head waitress and liked to take charge. Gemma could see how Scott probably appreciated the weight being lifted off him somewhat, especially the keeping people in line part. Although Gemma didn't understand why Janine did that (it wasn't like she was getting paid extra or even had a title), she was just naturally bossy and liked to take charge, Gemma presumed. She had no idea how the other staff dealt with her. Scott regularly came home with stories of Janine and other waitresses bickering about stupid crap. Because that's what it seemed like to Gemma—stupid crap.

She didn't like it how Scott would take Janine's phone calls the day after she'd had another fight with another one of her friends/waitresses. *Didn't Janine have any respect for anyone else's life?* Not everyone wanted to rehash her stupid childish arguments the next day. When she mentioned it to Scott, he just shrugged. He didn't really mind. Well, she did. It felt like Janine was muscling in on their lives. Her presence felt intrusive. *Doesn't she have her own husband to bitch and moan to?* She often thought she should say something to her, but when she really thought it through, she didn't see the point. What would she say anyway? Stop being so needy? Stop contacting my husband about everything that pops into your empty stupid head? Scott knew how she felt, he was an adult. It wasn't up to her to police his relationships with his staff. Gemma instead made a better effort to be in contact with Janine more, to get a better read on the situation. From her perspective and her knowledge of Scott, she wasn't really that concerned. Maybe they could be friends. It would certainly be convenient to have a friend on the street, even another family they could be friends with. Gemma didn't have any close girl friends here, so it was nice to have someone to talk to at times.

Gemma and Scott were back to being able to talk to each other relatively normally. He even told her his phone code. He said he had nothing to hide from her. This made her feel a little more comfortable, not that she was planning on going through his phone or anything. Their history stood them in good stead to just fall back into their easy communication. Besides if they were on the outs, Gemma wasn't ready to let go just yet. She still loved him deeply and still believed somewhere deep inside him (and her) that they were still meant to be together. And besides she was scared—scared of living without him. She usually shut that thought down as soon as it started. She didn't know where they were headed, but she was fairly sure it wasn't to separate. For so long, it felt like they were only at the beginning of their story. She didn't think it felt over yet. When she would tell Scott how she felt, he would listen, but wouldn't reply, beyond "You know I still love you Gem." But she quietly questioned that, she knew how it felt to be honestly and fully loved by him and didn't feel like that anymore.

Occasionally, they would still make love, which was always comforting and reassuring for her. Their bodies still fit together perfectly. A couple of times though, he'd say he would join her, and she would wake up alone. He would be passed out on the couch. Later he would say he was just so tired, had so much on at work, and that he'd "make it up to her." When he used to say that years ago, she knew he would be planning something, but now she heard it so often, she would just feel let down when he said it.

One morning, after Scott had gotten home late again, Gemma went into the spare room to wake him up. She saw his phone on the floor and picked it up.

As she turned it over, the screen lit up, and she saw a notification—a text message preview from Janine. She caught part of it.

"You know it kills me that we can't be together. I love you more than anything. This is our last chance to be together. We are destined, we belong together. I know you feel it too."

Gemma caught her breath. *What?*

She unlocked his phone and went to his text messages. Three of them—1:45 a.m., 2:20 a.m. and 3:05 a.m.—all confessing her undying love for him and telling him how there was no need for him to deny it any longer...

Gemma scrolled thru his messages. He had seen the first two. Thank God there was no reply from him. Small comfort. He had obviously gotten the last one after he'd come home and crashed out. She knew he would have gotten them while he was out last night.

Gemma felt her stomach drop to the floor and her throat tighten. *OMG, what on earth? Was he having a fling with this crazy bitch? Had they been carrying on right in front of her the whole time?* She read the messages one more time and took a deep breath, *Okay, it sounded like a desperate plea for Scott to be with her,* at least it didn't sound like something was already going on. She scrolled back through his message history with her, looking for anything untoward. She was relieved even though there were a lot of text messages, sometimes dozens a day about stupid random crap, but it was all legit (okay, crazy Janine stuff, but nothing intimate). She also noticed her text messages to him were usually long and involved, whereas his answers and replies were usually only a fraction of what she would write to him.

She put his phone back down and left the room. As she walked back down the hall, Gemma made an effort to keep breathing, in and out, in and out. She felt like all the blood was draining out of her body. A million questions bubbled up, making her throat tighten.

What was she supposed to do now? Was he planning on having an affair and didn't want to tell her (well, duh? Does any guy planning on having an affair ever actually "want" to tell his wife?) *Had he actually had a fling with her?* She didn't think so. She was sure she would have been able to tell, but OMG, had she missed the signs? Scott had always taken pride in his appearance, being a bar tender was like being on stage, much like her own job, being in front of the public required a higher level of personal grooming. Honestly she had put it down to him wanting to be relevant with his younger staff. Gemma hadn't thought anything of him asking her for face washing product advice. After all, he was also getting into his forties, but Scott would be eternally the good-looking bad boy/smart ass. Typical, men get distinguished and sexier, women get judged and over looked.

Should she go and wake him up and yell and make a scene?

No, that was not her style.

She got herself a glass of water and went back down to his room, shook him gently to wake him up. She asked if he was awake and then walked out of the room.

She had to get Noah up and get herself ready for work too. She had a fully booked makeup event today and couldn't afford to be ragged and distracted. She forced herself to take more deep breaths and get into the shower. It was going to be a long day.

Scott was in the kitchen by the time she was out of the shower. She couldn't even look at him. He asked her if anything was wrong. She shook her head. "I've got a big day ahead. Just getting my head in the game."

Gemma moved through her morning like a robot, stilted and stunned, feeling hollow and sick. Was Scott cheating on her? The feeling of some other woman scoping him out, declaring undying love for him was more than she could handle.

She knew they weren't getting on, but she never actually dreamed he would be shopping around for a new partner. Surely not. Was she deceiving herself? Was he deceiving her?

She was sure that she would have picked up on anything weird going on between her man and Janine.

Gemma didn't know what to think. Her head was spinning, and she wanted to run away.

Somehow autopilot kicked in, and she managed to get through her day, glad to throw herself into the busy-ness of women and makeup and beauty. She hardly took a break all day. When she did get a chance to take a breath, she checked her phone.

Scott had sent her a couple of texts asking about her day and letting her know he would be home that evening.

She would confront him about it tonight. No, she'd ask him. Ask for his side of the story. No, she'll not let on that she saw the text messages and ask leading questions, see what he voluntarily offered. No, she would confront Janine about the text messages. She should have taken screenshots them and sent them to her phone. She should have replied pretending to be Scott, telling her to back off. She would talk to Daniel and tell him what she found. No, she should talk to Scott first. She should check his phone regularly in case there were other messages from Janine.

Round and round her thoughts went.

The friends she had at work mentioned she looked terrible, but in a just-found-out-your-dog-died kind of way. Gemma just laughed, making a mental note to work on her facial expressions! Everyone always said she was so easy to read. Although luckily, most people are so self-centered, it's easy to change the subject by asking them about themselves, and ta-da, attention diverted.

It seemed like forever until after dinner. Scott kept trying to joke around and ask Gemma what was wrong. She'd just shrug and say they needed to talk. Finally when Noah was busy watching his favorite video, Gemma could sit down with Scott. Noah tended to get nervous when Gemma and Scott were alone together, like he was scared they would start fighting again. This made Gemma feel awful, and it hurt her heart that her little boy felt compelled to insert himself and be the peacekeeper. It could also be somewhat annoying as sometimes she needed to talk to Scott adult to adult. It didn't seem like there was much time anymore to ever talk to each other about anything.

The TV was loud enough to drown out their conversation at the breakfast bar.

"So tell me about you and Janine," Gemma started.

"What?" Scott answered, looking confused, then, "Oh my god, Gemma, did you read those text messages from her from last night?"

"Yes," Gemma answered.

"Honey, you have to believe me when I tell you they aren't anything. She bugs me all the time, and I always tell her no, but I guess last night she was super drunk and well, you saw…" He reached over and put his hand on her arm.

"What do you mean she bugs you all the time?" Gemma leaned in a little closer as Noah was eyeing them suspiciously from the living room. "She throws herself at you all the time?" Gemma suddenly thought of all the late-night drinking after work and wondered how many times it was just her and him. God, was he that freaking stupid? Yes.

"No. Lord, no, she's totally not my type (as if that was supposed to make her feel better). Just that, she is continually blowing up my phone about all sorts of stupid things." Scott seemed exasperated. "I've never said or done anything to make her think there was anything between her and I, but she just doesn't get it."

"Well by letting her text you and call you at all hours of the day and night, you kind of have let her think you're interested. Did you ever think about that? Have you actually ever said, 'Back off, I'm married'?" Gemma knew the answer before he answered. Of course not. He just shook his head but said nothing.

She went on, "Do you want me to call her and tell her to back off?"

"No," Scott replied.

"Well, I'm going to text her at least. Her behavior toward you is totally uncool. Should I tell Daniel?"

"Good god, no, it's hard enough to keep a balance on my staff. Anyway, he's super jealous, I don't want him thinking I'm trying to steal his wife or anything. They are having enough troubles."

How does he know Daniel is super jealous? How is he having conversations with Janine where that sort of topic is even coming up?

"Scott, have you been telling Janine about the troubles in our marriage?"

He looked sheepish. "Well, not exactly…"

"What do you mean 'not exactly'?" Gemma took a deep breath in. Was he really so clueless? Or was he just playing dumb? She thought he actually was that clueless. Good ole affable, charming Scott, never wanting to offend anyone—the excessive alcohol consumption definitely didn't help.

Again she found herself wondering if alcohol actually caused brain damage.

Scott paused for a while, looking down. "Look, she's such a great worker but very needy. I've never done or said anything to make her think there would ever be a chance, and she's freaking crazy! It's just easier to get along with her than not."

Gemma understood what he was saying, and besides, she was sure Janine made him feel important and great—obviously not the way he felt at home.

"Honey, I don't want to hurt you. I still love you." He reached for her hand. She let him take it. Gemma sighed. *What a mess.* She was so confused. She wanted to believe him. What he was saying felt right and truthful. Or she wanted to believe it felt that way.

"I still love you too." She looked at him. "I miss you, I miss us."

They didn't say anything for a while, just staring at each other.

"What are we going to do?" She sighed again.

He leaned forward so that their heads were touching. "I don't know, I miss you too. Why don't we see if we can go away somewhere together?"

Gemma felt herself perk up. "Really? That would be awesome! Where could we go? Can you get the time off work? Who will look after Noah?" Gemma bubbled over with excitement and questions.

Scott laughed and held up a hand. "We can figure it out."

Gemma felt the old comforting feeling so familiar from their past, their history together. So often when they'd be stuck, not knowing which way to go next, Scott would hug her and say, "We can figure it out," and then everything would be okay—or used to be. She had a small tinge of not really being sure this time but decided not to give in to it. He wanted to go away with her somewhere, and she wanted to be taken somewhere, that's all that mattered. A chance to reconnect.

But first, Janine. "Scott, give me your phone."

He looked puzzled. "Why?"

"I'm going to text Janine and tell her to back off. If she won't take the hint from you, I'll just have to remind her that you're married."

"Okay." Scott handed her his phone. "Don't be too mean though, I still have to work with her."

"I know, why don't you fire her?"

"For what? Having a crush on the boss? Seriously, Gem, I wouldn't have any staff."

Gemma laughed in spite of herself. Scott was never deficient in the self-esteem department.

Gemma opened Scott's text messages but didn't see anything from Janine. She looked at Scott.

"Yeah, I deleted them," he said, answering her question before she even asked it.

"Have you spoken to her today?"

"Only at work."

"Did she say anything?"

"No, she was starting her shift as I was finishing up with Sooz." Gemma knew every week, he would have a meeting with the heads of each department separately.

"Okay."

Gemma took a few minutes, thinking of the right way to say what she wanted to say.

"Janine, it's Gemma. I read your text messages to Scott. Back off, totally inappropriate. Leave him alone. I will send them to Daniel if I see anything else from you."

She hit send and breathed a heavy sigh.

Within a few minutes, Janine texted Gemma's phone. "I'm so sorry, can we talk?"

Gemma didn't answer for a couple of hours. She just sent one word back: "tomorrow."

Janine texted her immediately. "What time?"

"Afternoon."

Scott looked relieved and put his arm around her, planting a kiss on her forehead. "Let's just hang out tonight, I don't want to talk about this anymore."

Gemma had no argument with that. She was sick of Janine imposing on their time, home, and headspace. She was a piece of work for sure.

Gemma and Scott hung out the rest of the night like old times. They watched a movie with Noah, and she let Scott sleep with her. They just held each other. Gemma had strange disconcerting dreams of flooding and tidal waves and being swept away. Feelings of powerlessness and futility invaded her sleep. When she woke up, she prayed and meditated, then while everyone was still asleep, she went for a run to clear her head.

She made sure she went down the street in the opposite direction of Janine's house. Ugh. Why was she having to deal with this?

And what exactly was this? Scott had never doubted her intuition before. Was he in denial of anything himself or just lying to her? She hated that she was even questioning his intentions and that she felt uneasy about the whole situation.

As Gemma ran, she thought about God and why he let crappy things happen to good people. Was she a good person? Wasn't Scott a good person too? As she fell into a steady pace, she prayed for wisdom, for clarity, for courage. She felt heavy and like the rug was being pulled out from under her in slow motion, knowing it was happening and not being able to do anything about it. Still, she prayed as she ran, feeling a little more comfort but very alone.

Chapter 12

White Girl Drunk

That afternoon took a long time to arrive. Scott had come home after doing most of his ordering (which he never did) and then headed back to work for a meeting. Noah had been invited to a friend's house for a play date. Just as she was getting home from dropping Noah off, Janine called. Gemma felt instantly nervous. What would she say? She gave herself a quick pep talk—she was fully within her rights to defend her relationship and tell the crazy bitch to back off. Who did she think she was anyway?

After the awkward hellos, Gemma jumped right in. "So what's your deal, Janine? Why are you sending my husband undying love text messages? Do you do this with every dude you work with or just mine?"

There was an awkward pause, and Gemma wondered momentarily if she was still there.

"Oh wow, are you sure they were for Scott? And not for Daniel? We've been going to counselling, and I thought they would probably have been meant for him."

Gemma was not expecting that answer. What the freak was she playing at?

"Um, yes, you used his name." She put on a stupid voice. "'We are meant to be together, Scott. This is your last chance, Scott. We are destined to be together, Scott.' Would you like me to go on?"

Janine muttered a "Nope" and paused, changing tactic.

"Are you sure they were from me? Because I don't have them on my phone."

"Are you messing with me right now?" Gemma was pissed. Did she think she could just play stupid and Gemma would buy it? Really? "And why are you even texting Scott so late at night? Do you text everyone after midnight? You know he's married and has a family."

"He's just a good friend, I don't know. I've got a new phone. I'm not really sure how it even works properly yet. I don't even remember. I'm so sorry, I was so drunk. I was like white girl drunk. He's just such a good friend. I'm sorry." Janine was backpedaling and talking fast. Gemma didn't know whether to be confused or insulted. Was she apologizing for writing the text messages or just because Gemma found them?

What the hell was white girl drunk? Sounds like got-a-problem-with-binge-drinking-like-a-college-kid drunk. Does that make incredibly inappropriate behavior okay? Who is this chick? What parallel universe was she living in where she thought it was okay to text her boss after midnight about anything?

"Well, you need to back the hell off my husband, whatever your excuse is! Seriously, Janine, you're a married woman, an adult with children. You can't just get wasted and then plead drunkenness as an excuse," Gemma hissed at her. "Does that shit work for you often? Do you usually develop inappropriate crushes on your boss? What is your problem? Back off!"

"No, of course not, I am so sorry," Janine gushed. "It will never happen again."

"It had better not. I think I'll just send these messages to Daniel. Maybe I should do that anyway." She felt a strange satisfaction hearing Janine gasp.

"Please don't!"

Gemma didn't actually save the text messages. She was so stunned when she read them she didn't think to send them to her phone.

Gemma ended the call, momentarily missing the days when you could slam down the phone. Besides, she didn't know what else to say. She'd never been in this situation before. What the hell were you supposed to say? She hated confrontations but wasn't afraid to speak up if she had to, especially if someone was sniffing around her husband. Really, so they might be having troubles, but they were still married. They had never had an "open" marriage, and Gemma wasn't about to start! Even if Scott wasn't wearing a wedding ring and wasn't acting like her husband, didn't mean he wasn't *her* husband. That didn't make her feel any less awkward. The whole situation sucked. She felt resentful that he even put her in this position.

She realized she still believed deep down that marriage was for life—one man, one woman, together forever, in sickness and in health. To be respected by each person in the marriage *and* by those around them. *Holy crap, if you are around a bunch of people that don't have any respect for the institute of marriage and you aren't so sure yourself because of your bad habits, then what hope do you have?* Was she fighting a losing battle?

Should she have just trusted Scott to deal with the issue on his own?

Well, she knew he wouldn't. He hated conflict even more than her. He hated being the bad guy and didn't deal very well with adversity. Gemma genuinely believed that he still wanted to be with her and be a family. She still held true to the fact that he was her man, her human, together forever to love one another. Right?

Suddenly Gemma had a slim insight into his mindset. Anything to avoid the brutality of the real world, he just wanted to be the good time guy, always and forever—good time Dad, good time husband, good time boss, good time Scott. The ultimate fair weather friend. Gemma was surprised at this thought. For so long, she had been under the spell of a perfect life together, she had never really thought of him critically before. She quickly pushed it into the corner of her mind.

Good grief, she didn't really enjoy dealing with this crap either, but Janine needed to *back off*. No one weaseled their way into her relationship or family.

Although Gemma did feel a little insecure, was this somehow her fault? Was Scott losing his attraction to her because she was getting into her forties now? She had noticed that she was changing, not exactly the young, high-spirited, impulsive chick she once was. There were wrinkles and grey hairs slowly becoming more noticeable. Was the fact that she was a little older than him suddenly not attractive to him anymore? She hadn't let herself go or anything, she was proud of herself that in the years since Noah was born, she had found a peace and appreciation for her body she had never experienced before.

She stopped herself with a laugh. Of all the futile things to worry about, aging and the weather were probably top of the list. She couldn't even bring herself to get on that sad and sorry track. She had grown and given birth to a beautiful healthy baby boy. Her body was amazing! It had been a faithful friend, and she was done chastising and criticizing it.

Gemma knew this, but still…

He was surrounded by a bunch of kids in their late twenties and early thirties still in the party time of their lives. Somehow Gemma thought that the natural evolution of their relationship had bought them to a comfortable happy place where they could see their dreams and goals come to fruition. How could she be so wrong?

What did Scott want?

Until recently, their communication had been open and honest. Until recently…

Who knew, maybe this was the shake-up their relationship needed? Although she could think of slightly less painful ways to shake up a relationship. Was that what this was about? Scott was bored with her and their relationship? She didn't think so, but not wearing his wedding ring and barely being available for her or Noah was sending some pretty strong signals. They really had a lot to talk about. She craved the honest conversations they used to have, right up until…when? Right about three or four months after they moved here, when his drinking really took on a life of its own and he surrounded himself with a bunch of new cool kids that didn't know Scott and Gemma, they only knew Scott, and he didn't care that they had only a passing knowledge of his wife and child—like they weren't actually real.

Good grief, are all men really insecure and spineless when it comes down to it? She felt her heart snap closed and suddenly understood all the women she had met who had hardened their hearts with bitterness to all men because of the actions of one. Wow, she couldn't let herself do that either!

Gemma took a couple of deep breaths and prayed. Maybe sharing this burden with God would ease her heart and mind, but she was never really sure if she ever was "giving it to God" correctly. She concentrated on imagining her heart staying open. The image she had was that it was a giant clam shell like the one in the vestibule of the Catholic church she grew up attending. It was positioned inside of the entrance to the church that held holy water so that you could bless yourself before you entered the nave. As a child, it was always so interesting to her. She often wondered where it had come from, seeing as they were so far away from the ocean. It was thick, and you could see the layers where the shell had grown over time. It was smooth and white on the inside, and she used to daydream in those long church services about the size of the pearl that must have come out of it.

When Scott got home later, they talked about her conversation with Janine. Scott seemed interested (and why wouldn't he be?) although he seemed to want to check again that she wasn't too mean to Janine. He asked again if he should fire her. She laughed. *For what?* Gemma questioned herself. *Having a crush on the boss?* When she broke it down to what it really was, it sounded so minor and ridiculous, except to her—to her, it felt like an earthquake. She was shaken and was working very hard to keep perspective.

Scott agreed he would keep Janine at arm's length. Gemma wondered where he had been keeping her before.

She was genuinely tired of this whole situation and decided to believe him based on their history and that she had known him in so many situations for almost twenty years. This was one of the best one-on-one nights she'd had with him for a while.

It felt like home, the way he had always made her feel. She actually felt like Scott was interested in her. It was a comforting feeling that she'd had for a long time and felt so much like home she actually relaxed for a little while.

They talked about how their lives were, what they were experiencing and going through. They laughed and remembered fun previous experiences they'd had together. Scott suggested they get away together for a three-day weekend, that they hadn't had any time as a couple together, that he missed her too.

Even Noah was comfortable. He kept looking over from the TV as if he couldn't quite fathom how peaceful they were being. When it was time, he went to bed without a fuss and left them to hang out and talk. When Gemma checked on him, he was sound asleep snuggled with Gary, who was almost on the pillow with him.

Gemma felt happy and secure, although in the back of her mind, she kept pushing down the growing cynicism and doubts she had. She desperately wanted to believe his sweet-talking wide-eyed promises. She was confused. For so long *this* had been Scott. Why should she be so quick to throw away all history because of a rough year or so? It seemed he believed what he was saying. Despite everything, she knew him better than anyone. She just wanted everything to be back to the way they had been for almost two decades. Maybe they had let the heat be turned down too long on their frying pan. Maybe she needed to turn it up a little—remind him of the amazing woman she was and that she was his.

They set a date for a month away, and that night after they made love in the familiar sensual way she had missed for months, Gemma slept better. She felt like they had come closer again, instead of the far apart that was so commonplace. Again they slept in each other's arms, but her dreams were not disturbing and frightening. It was the best sleep she'd had in ages although when she woke up, she had a strange sense that all of this was temporary.

In the quiet house before everyone else awoke, Gemma kneeled at the end of her bed and prayed. She prayed for strength to keep her heart open. She prayed for courage to keep believing in her husband and their union. She prayed for wisdom to not give in to her insecurities, to know when it was her intuition and not her paranoia. But most of all, she prayed for Scott that he find his way back to being a good, honest man, faithful husband, and doting father.

She felt hopeful that maybe *this time* would be different. They probably just needed time to reconnect and remember how much they loved to be together and remember all their hopes and dreams and ideas that they'd shared for so long.

She wanted to believe that was all they needed to get back on track. She could barely admit to herself that she was probably wrong.

PART 3

The End Is Not Goodbye

Chapter 13

Deeper Still

The following Sunday, the learning series was a new one—a short four-week series on prayer. Gemma read the screens before the service started, somewhat interested but lost in her own thoughts, and didn't really take any of it in. The sermon was about how we often don't ask God for what we really want, that we keep ourselves in our difficult circumstances because of how we pray.

This immediately got Gemma's attention. She thought of how often she prayed for wisdom and courage and strength, how many times a day she did it, and that God kept giving her more situations to build her wisdom, courage, and strength! She nearly laughed out loud at the simplicity of the message. It had never occurred to her that by doing so, God was actually giving her more circumstances in which she needed wisdom, courage, and strength.

She could barely contain herself with this realization.

She made up her mind right then to pray for grace, peace, and joy instead and see how that worked out.

The sermon the pastor was sharing, also talked about how the enemy is waiting constantly to interfere in our families. Even though Gemma was familiar with the "enemy," she had never really considered that he could have an impact on her life. Why her little old insignificant life? She was about as regular and normal as anyone. Why would the devil want to interfere with *her* life? But the more she thought about it, the more she also realized that her family situation was prime for the enemy's intrusion. He had entered and was destroying their family bond and love. That was how he worked, disrupting harmony and peace, and getting rid of love, replacing it with suspicion and resentment.

Even as she thought this, she realized that anyone she spoke to about this would consider her to be a crazy person!

She sounded like her own mother! Gemma had a momentary wish that she could confide in her mom. She could do with someone who had her back at the moment. She knew it wouldn't be her family though. She could almost hear her mother's disapproving, judgmental tone, either telling her to work harder to be a better wife or reprimanding her for not keeping God front and center in their marriage and what did she expect from marrying a non-Christian, blah blah blah. Probably best she didn't think about that too much.

That was definitely something she was keeping on the down low. She would change her prayer language and requests and start petitioning the Lord with more direct prayer requests. Gemma was feeling closer to God than she had in a long time, like she actually understood a bit more of how this "faith" thing worked.

Yes. That's what she would do.

She thought back to her last conversation with Celia, about God being love in everything. God was present when there was love, so it made sense that the enemy would want to get rid of love anywhere he could with the help of the seven deadly sins—envy, gluttony, greed, lust, pride, sloth, and wrath. Wow, Gemma felt like a light had just been turned on and almost felt ashamed recognizing how many of these things had crept into her life and relationship. But instead of giving into shame, which would be letting the enemy still have influence, she made a conscious decision that it would be okay. Amazed at her new perspective and how even though at various points in her life she felt she had already experienced insight into these life lessons, now she was gaining a deeper, wider perspective.

Gemma sat in the darkness of the church and let the tears roll down her face, quietly grateful for the anonymity of the dark peaceful room. She really felt safe here, at peace. It was a welcome respite from her life "out there." The opportunity to listen and think about the bigger picture was akin to meditation for her. She often wished she could convince Scott to come along. Noah adored the adults who took the children's ministry, especially the older retired ones. He also loved hanging out with the other kids. Gemma often wondered what sort of relationship Noah would have had with either set of his grandparents if they had lived closer to them or they had been "traditional" in their roles the way she remembered her grandparents being.

*****

The week or so after the "text message" incident, they talked about their weekend away almost every day—where they would go, who would look after Noah and Gary. Scott realized, however, that Marshside Mama's had a job fair the weekend that they had planned to go away, and then the sitter Gemma had lined up for the following weekend to take care of Noah and Gary had something come up. Gemma herself had a weekend event after that. It kept getting pushed further and further back.

They kept clinging to the idea though.

Scott's schedule was still as hectic as ever, as luck would have it (or not, as the case maybe) the restaurant was ridiculously busy *all* the time. It was a valuable reflection on Scott and his management team that they had a dedicated group of core staff who worked well together as a single unit. But they needed more help. Job fairs were something that needed his attention. He had found that over time if he put in the effort at the very beginning of the hiring process, it really paid off in staff longevity.

This did not bode well for Gemma and Noah, however. Even though Scott was marginally more present physically and seemed to spend less time drinking and passing out fully clothed on the couch, he wasn't very present emotionally when he was home—phone always in hand, some emergency constantly demanding his attention. Before she knew it, nearly two months had gone by with barely a mention of the supposed weekend away pinned down.

Whenever she would mention it, she would get one of Scott's famous winks. "I can't wait, honey, but let me get through this week/

catastrophe/owners' meeting/training." There was always something demanding his time and attention. Gemma kept praying for grace, peace, and joy. On one hand, she kind of felt a bit miffed that he didn't seem to be placing their marriage as a priority. On the other hand, she understood he was pulled in so many directions constantly. She didn't really want to make it worse.

Still, she told herself it was a wife's duty to be there and support her husband in his time of need, not to be too needy herself. She didn't really buy the submissive wife crap though. That had never been her MO. She and Scott had always been partners, together for each other. When one was weak, the other strong; one down, the other would bring them up. So with that in mind, she did her best to be understanding and supportive; however, she felt more and more invisible to him, like a piece of the furniture. And it killed her to watch him brush Noah off after he would promise him movies or other activities. Was God teaching her the art of the slow simmer? Or should she be turning up the heat?

One evening, Gemma asked him point-blank if he still wanted to go away with her. He started with all kinds of promises and professions of love, but he saw the look in her eyes and heaved a heavy sigh. "No, honey. I don't honestly see how I'm going to pull it off. I'm so busy right now, I'm sorry." He pulled her close to him, and she breathed in his familiar scent.

"Okay." She withdrew from his embrace, looking up at him, feeling slightly annoyed at his response. Did he not remember who she was? How well they knew each other? She felt like he was just saying words to appease her. "Do you want to spend any time with me at all?"

"Of course, Gem." He kissed her forehead. "I'm just so busy with work. You know what it's like." He implored, "How about I take you out for dinner instead? We could make a night of it, organize a sleepover for Noah, go somewhere for appetizers, then we could go to a restaurant on the other side of town where I don't know anyone and we won't be bothered or interrupted? Just me and you? Like old times." He raised his eyebrows at her, cupping her face.

She looked into his eyes, looking for…what? Or was it who was she looking for? The husband she was holding out for? Was he actually coming back? Was he still in there?

Gemma remained hopeful. Deep down, her prevailing belief was still that marriage was a lifetime commitment, till death do they part.

"Well, it's better than nothing I guess," she replied, trying not to sound disappointed. Although she sounded to her own ears more disappointed than she meant to, Scott didn't seem to pick up on it.

"Great, babe, why don't you buy yourself something new to wear? I don't mind, go treat yourself." He kissed her on the lips—a quick peck as he turned back to his phone, continuing, "I'll make the reservations if you want, just name the place."

Gemma thought quickly. "Um…" Scott interrupted her though with excitement, he put down his phone. "How about that new French place that just opened recently?" She'd heard some of the girls at work talking about it. Run by a French family, the food was divine along with the wine. Surely there wouldn't be anyone Scott knew there. Gemma nodded, catching his excitement.

"Perfect, babe, I'm on it. How's Saturday next week?" He glanced in her direction then glanced at his phone.

"Sounds awesome." She smiled at him. He wasn't looking.

But that did sound awesome. She never got to go out and eat anywhere or dress up or feel important to anyone her own age anymore.

Gemma loved that she got to spend so much time with Noah, but sometimes she just wanted—no, she craved some adult time. A glass of wine with a girlfriend or a massage, a night off without feeling guilty—something for herself.

She understood though, with all the uncertainty in his life at present, it was very important to Noah to know he had at least *one* parent he could rely on, and honestly Gemma didn't feel she had any friends that she was that close to anyway.

The whole process of "finding" new girlfriends was an unpredictable journey that Gemma felt useless at. Sure, she'd made friends with different moms through Noah's various activities, but like herself, they all worked, and with so many different schedules, it was a genuine mission to find a time she could get together with any of them. Again, she thought of how easy it had been to make friends whilst in a "happy" relationship. Let's face it, by this point in life, all the singles their age stuck together, all the married couples stuck together, and the divorced ones stuck to themselves anyway.

It would be good to just go out and be Gemma for a change. Not Mom.

Chapter 14

Dinner Date

The following week came quickly. Gemma had organized Noah to have a sleepover at a friend's place and bought herself a new dress—something not too skin-tight but still sexy, skimming all the right curves with a little cleavage. She had never really bought the idea that sexy was wearing something so tight it left little to the imagination. She had always thought sexy was more about creating a little mystery. Scott used to think so as well, although these days she wasn't so sure. It obviously wasn't something followed a lot around here, especially not with the crew Scott worked with. Was she just getting older and more intolerant of slutty dressing? No, she had never gone for the painted-on clothing look. It just wasn't her style.

She knew Scott had never been impressed with the women who wore their clothes two sizes too small. They had always joked that these girls had better develop a personality before they lost their gorgeous figures because once they lost everything they had going for them, they would be left with nothing.

They headed over to the French restaurant, making small talk about their week and what Noah was up to at school. Just before they got out of the car, Scott grabbed Gemma's hand and turned toward her. "You look great, babe. I'm sorry we couldn't go away." He seemed like he actually regretted it, Gemma thought hopefully. "Let's enjoy the time we can have together."

Gemma felt herself blush. She looked down nervously (although she didn't know why she was blushing!). "That's a great idea," she agreed, kissing the back of his hand. "You look pretty hot yourself." She winked at him, because he did. He was wearing a blue plaid button down shirt that was open at the neck with dark blue chinos, his salt-and-pepper hair styled in a faux hawk. He was clean shaven and smelt divine.

"Well, babe, I just gotta keep up with you." He gave her a sexy up-and-down glance and winked back.

It was an unexpected and sincere moment. She was flattered and felt nervous. *Do I have butterflies right now?* The question left her mind as quickly as it had entered.

The restaurant was small but incredibly intimate and well thought out for the long narrow space, with discrete booth seating staggered down each side. Each booth had luxurious satin, lace and delicate ribbon pillows and mini hanging chandeliers casting soft shadows in each one, creating a dozen magical islands of privacy and confidentiality. There may have been people in some of them, but Gemma didn't notice, she was completely enthralled. The walls were painted like a Parisian street scene, drawing the eye to the end of the room and an accurate yet romantic version of the Eiffel tower. The ceiling was painted like the early evening sky, soft deep twilight tones fading to an inky indigo in the center of the ceiling. It was so well done, they were truly transported to another place. The music was French cafe/musette, the lighting gentle and soft. Gemma loved it. She stood still for a second, taking it all in.

Scott slipped his arm around her waist. "Do you like it? I thought of you as soon as I heard about this place."

"Oh, honey, I love it," she whispered, feeling her eyes widen trying to take in every magical detail.

Their waiter greeted them at the host stand and ushered them to their booth. There was a bottle of French champagne waiting for them at the table in an elaborate ice bucket. The champagne flutes were tall and narrow, delicate stems with art nouveau-styled glasswork etched around the base of the glasses, standing side by side, looking more like a fine art installation than tableware.

Scott took Gemma's wrap. As he did, he leaned in close to her and whispered, "I hope you like it."

She looked at him, catching for a moment the old genuine hopeful Scott she knew and missed so much. He looked at her with so much genuine anticipation, she felt for a moment she might cry with gratitude. Gemma suddenly felt like she might burst, her love for him overwhelming her. She caught herself and replied with a breathless "It's perfect!"

He handed her wrap to the waiter as he guided her to one side of the booth with his hand on the small of her back. It was a simple but loving gesture. She slid into the booth still with eyes wide, trying to absorb it all, Scott took the champagne bottle with a flourish as he slid into the seat opposite her, pouring them a glass each. He handed her one as he put the bottle back into its bucket and took his glass. He raised it. "To the most amazing woman I know."

She felt herself blush again. Not wanting to ruin the moment, she just smiled at him. They spent a long moment staring into each other's eyes.

As they took a sip of champagne, real champagne that was effervescent and light tickling her nose, she felt bubbly herself. "This place is amazing!" she exclaimed. "It's like we could almost be back in Paris."

"I know, right?" he replied.

"Except we're not lost and starving and exhausted. Remember that ridiculous day?" She laughed. Scott reminisced with her and laughed too.

When they were in London, they had decided to take a weekend trip to Paris by just catching the train through the channel tunnel, which was easy, but when in France, they had ended up getting on a wrong train and on the wrong side of Paris. They had figured they could just walk to the cheap hotel they had made a reservation at using a handheld GPS they had just bought in London. Seemed like a simple enough plan. Except they had lost the address of the hotel and only knew part of the name, they ended up walking for hours around Paris, trying to use the Eiffel Tower as their landmark. As the afternoon dragged into early evening and their patience and stomachs were being tested, they found a café on the edge of the Champ de Mars Park where they had decided to just stop and get something to eat. The sun was setting as they shared a bottle of wine and waited for their food to arrive, the stress of the last few hours disappeared as they laughed at their unfortunate luck and settled into the atmosphere of the quaint café. The owners of the cafe had turned out to be a wonderfully friendly couple named Fred and Adeline who had recently returned from Park City, Utah, where Scott and Gemma had been living and had even eaten at the restaurant Scott worked at. After filling their bellies and drinking a few more glasses of wine with Fred and Adeliene, who pointed them in the right direction of the hotel, they headed out into the night, re-energized. They had wandered around the Champ de Mars in the dark, following the path of romantic lamps that lit the way, arm in arm, enjoying the ambience, each other, and the buzz from the wine, they strolled in step together, more in love than ever. Scott joked that there was no one else he would rather be unwashed with. Gemma agreed. They had each other and that was all that mattered.

"*That* was a crazy adventure, wasn't it? How lucky were we that we met Fred and Adeliene at that cafe? I knew I had married the right girl then." Scott grinned momentarily lost in the memory. His attention was bought back quickly however, by a buzz from his phone, he took it out of his pocket and looked at it briefly.

"Really?" she asked. "I thought you were leaving it at home or in the car." Gemma could hear the hurt in her voice.

"Really what? I can look at my phone, I'm the GM you know. What if something happens at work? I need to stay on top of it." His tone was excusatory and slightly defensive, like he didn't see anything wrong with his behavior.

"I thought it was just going to be us, you and me, not you, me, and your phone…" Gemma trailed off. She looked down and took a deep breath, struggling to remain in control of her emotions.

Scott stared at her for a moment and sighed. "Okay, honey, I'm sorry." He genuinely looked apologetic. "Just habit, I guess. I just don't want to blow it at work. There will be no more phone or work for the rest of the night, scout's honor." He gave a half-hearted Boy Scout salute and put his phone down on the seat beside him.

She barely managed a token smile, still irrationally consumed with emotion, feeling like a little kid struggling to keep an adult's attention.

Gemma felt deflated and incredibly disappointed, like she might just burst into tears. She made the observation that she was so emotionally fragile at the moment she felt like a yo-yo, swept away with romance, hope, and anticipation one minute, on the verge of tears the next. *Great. What is happening to me? This isn't the me I thought I knew.* She didn't really even know who she was anymore because she really didn't. This thought troubled her, made her feel like she was drowning and couldn't get any air.

Scott was watching her. She wondered if he could still read her the way she could still read him. She honestly didn't know. She hardly recognized him when he looked at her these days, he seldom looked at her the way he used to anymore. It made her feel so distant from him, like she didn't really know him at all. This was one of those moments.

She took a deep breath and forced herself to smile. "I wonder what the bathrooms look like?"

Gemma excused herself to use the restroom. In the bathroom, she ran her wrists under cold water and stared at herself in the mirror, giving herself a pep talk. *Don't blow it, girl. You've been waiting for some alone time with him for months, just enjoy it. It'll be fun. He still loves you, right? He's here now, isn't he?* Gemma couldn't argue with that logic, reminding herself that he had planned this romantic dinner, for them to spend some time together.

She touched up her lipstick, patted away a few stray strands of hair, and smiled at herself in the mirror. Her strange grimace actually caused her to laugh bringing her back to the present moment. She seized that moment to head back to the table. Feeling more confident, she came back to the booth. Scott was studying the menu. She brushed her hand across his shoulder as she walked past and sidled back onto her side on the table.

"What do you think?" she asked Scott.

He smiled at her. "Do you want me to order?"

"Sure, what will you delight my taste buds with?" She grinned back.

"Well, my lady," Scott continued with a twinkle, describing the wonderful appetizers followed by the entrée, and for dessert, they could head to Death by Chocolate—a coffee and dessert cafe not too far away—if they were up for it. He had even chosen the wine that would pair perfectly with the main course. He raised his glass to her, "Let's enjoy this!"

Gemma was suddenly hungry and looked forward to trying all the amazing food he had chosen for them. He poured them another glass of champagne as the waiter arrived and he ordered for them.

Gemma made a conscious effort to enjoy this time with him, and it was well worth it. They ate and drank and laughed and talked about their lives and Noah, plans for his birthday, and how crazy things had been for them both. Gemma felt for a moment like they were back to their old selves—she and him against the world, on their own island of love and direction.

She felt so far removed from what their everyday had become, it was like a weight had been lifted off her, even if just for a moment. Although when she reflected later, the champagne probably helped.

Before she knew it, they had eaten an appetizer and split the entrees, trying each other's the way they used to. They had drank another bottle of wine, and they ordered an after dinner port, pausing for a moment, looking at each other.

"Now what?" she asked him, not knowing what she wanted to do next. She just knew she didn't want this to end.

"Well, Death by Chocolate closes in fifteen minutes, so that's out." Gemma was surprised at how quickly the evening had gone. Scott started then caught himself.

"What?" Gemma asked. "What were you thinking?"

"We could go to that Japanese place we went to a few months ago? They're open late, and it's usually pretty quiet." Gemma had a fleeting thought of *Yeah, and all your workers hang out there*, but then she figured, who cares? She'd had just enough wine to actually be interested if they were there, to be able to watch Scott interact with them. If they were there, surely he wouldn't be asking her to go if he did have anything to hide

But she didn't want it to be awkward.

"I don't know, honey." She had doubts. After all she hadn't seen Janine since the text message incident and didn't really know if she wanted to have to deal with her if she was there. "Will Janine be there?" She looked sideways at him.

"I don't think so." He didn't miss a beat. "It's her night off, she doesn't usually go out if she's not working."

"Okay cool, let's go then," she said, thinking to herself that he seemed to know a lot about her movements, but she blew it off. Scott was still her husband, and he was with her tonight. He had planned this great night for the two of them. He was still her husband. That was it. She pushed Janine out of her mind, not wanting to let some stupid girl with an inappropriate crush on her husband ruin the remainder of the night or take up residence in her thoughts.

They left the French restaurant arm in arm. When they got to the car, Scott wrapped his arms around her, and they shared a long hug and a passionate kiss. How she loved his warm soft lips.

"I've missed you, Gemma."

She stared into his deep dark eyes. "I've missed you too. What's happening to us, Scott? Is our marriage broken?" She sighed.

"I don't know. I hope not," he replied as he opened her car door for her. "Whatever is happening sucks though."

She agreed as she got into the car but wondered what he meant by that. *Did he not think his actions had anything to do with the state of their marriage? Did he just think it was all out of his control?* She watched him and couldn't help but notice that he checked his phone as he walked around the car. He paused for a moment before he got in, scrolling and reading a text message obviously. When he got into the car, his whole vibe had changed. He didn't look like the dreamy sexy Scott who had just opened the car door for her. His face was contorted as if there was suddenly a whole lot going on in his world that he was trying to keep in.

"What's up?" Gemma asked.

"Oh, nothing," he lied.

"Come on, Scott, I saw you check your text messages. What's going on?" She put her hand on his arm. Pleading, she was aware of holding her breath.

Scott heaved a heavy sigh. Gemma felt the glow of the previous blissful moment slipping away, Scott's face was concerned. She felt nervous, a million bad thoughts ran through her head in that split second.

"Daniel's father and brother were in a car accident. His brother's dead, his father is being airlifted to Charlotte. Daniel left work and is headed there right now. Jacob is driving him. Daniel is an emotional wreck." Scott trailed off with his hands on the steering wheel, staring straight ahead. He hadn't started the car yet.

Gemma suddenly felt like she was spinning. She felt sabotaged and disappointed. She knew she had to pull it together and be a big girl about this though. This was serious. In the bigger picture, this outranked all. "Oh, wow, that's terrible! I'm so sorry, what a horrible thing to happen! Who's covering for him? Is he okay? Were any other family members involved?" It occurred to her she didn't know anything about Daniel's family. Was it big or little? Lots of siblings or just one? Like that made any difference. But in the back of her mind, she didn't really see what it had to do with Scott and their evening together. *Who texted him? Couldn't the MOD handle it?* She knew they had a very competent management team, why would they contact him right now as it happened? *Didn't he tell them it was a big night? Was it Janine? She just couldn't leave him alone for a night?? He must have told her he was taking me out for a romantic dinner, right? WTF?*

Gemma took a deep breath in, suddenly overwhelmed and defensive, wanting to rewind the last five minutes. She would have taken his phone away, kept him busy, focused on her so he wouldn't have glanced at this phone. She heard the quiver in her draw of breath.

Scott did too. He turned to her and put his hand over hers. "It's okay, hon, Jacob was going with him."

Gemma realized he thought she was concerned about Daniel and his family. She felt a pang of guilt that it was purely a selfish moment. She didn't care what had happened to his employee's family, she cared about what this meant for their time together which they didn't have anymore. But yes, what a truly awful thing to have happen to anyone. She wouldn't wish that sort of thing on anybody. She also knew their night was over. Her thoughts were all over the place. She felt hot tears of disappointment welling in her eyes. She couldn't help but feel she'd just lost Scott.

Their night was done.

She couldn't help the sinking feeling that maybe their marriage was too.

This one thing seemed to her the most obvious glaring flaw in their present day relationship: Scott's time with Gemma was not coveted nor prioritized by him the way he used to, like the way she still did. He used to always make her the center of his attention. Whenever she called, dropped in to see him, even at home talking to each other, she never had any doubts that he was *with* her, because he was *there*—mind, body, and spirit. For seventeen years without missing a beat, he made her feel like she was his queen, and he, in turn, was her king. Not these days. Any prior time or attention he said he had for her was easily replaced in his mind (and heart) with anything else that may crop up—like anything.

She put her head into her hands, took another breath to regain control, and asked, "So what do you think we should do?" meaning with the rest of their plans for the night.

Scott took it a completely different way. "Well, Janine is at her house with the kids. Daniel and Jacob have already left. I'll have to call Mama's and see what's up."

So it was Janine who had sent him the text message. That was a lot of information to send in one message.

Then he added, "I guess we should just go home, and I'll see if Janine is okay."

"*What?*" Gemma asked incredulously, feeling the last scraps of dreamy romantic feelings ebb away.

He turned to look at her. "What do you mean 'What,' Gemma?"

"I mean, why does she need checking on? I'm sure she's probably already told everyone and has rallied all the sympathy she can generate. What are you going to do that can't wait till tomorrow?"

Scott stared at her. "Well, that's pretty heartless, Gem. I never picked you to be so mean-spirited." He looked disgusted.

Gemma felt completely wounded. She didn't understand how it was all turning to crap after it was all just awesome.

"Really? After all that shit she just put us through recently? I'm supposed to be supportive of you cutting short our date night, that we never get anymore, because her husband had a family tragedy and she's at home with the kids? Wouldn't she be planning on going up there too? Would you cut short a night with your wife for any other of your staff members who experienced a family tragedy?" She gave him an accusatory look. "I don't think so, Scott," she almost hissed the last words, surprising even herself.

"Oh my god, Gemma, *get over it!* It was just a stupid crush. I don't have any feelings for her beyond being a friend. She's a good friend, that's all. We have a few laughs together. She's fun to be around." Scott kept staring at her with that awful look on his face, Gemma had never seen him look at her like that before, ever.

She felt her thoughts spinning, trying to keep up with what was happening, trying to remain focused on her thoughts and feelings. This was so unfair! Her vision blurred as the hot tears spilled and ran down her cheeks. She wasn't looking at Scott anymore, she was staring straight ahead as he started the car. "Well, it didn't feel like a stupid crush to me, Scott. It felt like a very real and very close threat and a kick in the stomach that you refuse to take any responsibility for!" She blinked hard to keep more tears from falling, desperately trying to regain control of her emotions, her voice, her tears, her life.

"I can't control the way people feel about me!" he yelled at her. "Seriously? What is wrong with you? Why do you have to be so negative all the time?" he demanded, fuming.

Gemma said nothing, confused and hurt. She hung her head and cried silently, the tears making large wet splotches on the fabric of her dress.

She sat doubting herself, doubting her perceptions, her memories.

Was she a heartless person? Was she wrong in wanting to protect her time alone with Scott? He seemed to think so. Since when was he so fricking concerned with comforting anyone?

And there it was staring her in the face. He very definitely had feelings for Janine. At no other time in their relationship had he even put a family member in front of her. *He* would always be the one to turn off his phone whenever they went anywhere together, protecting their time and life together. Gemma wondered how she could have been so stupid and so blind.

Silently, she searched for God in her mind and heart, not wanting to turn into an emotional mess, searching for comfort in any recent thought or memory.

Too late with the mess part, she thought bitterly.

She was completely unraveling. It was suddenly all so horribly clear. Here she had been trying to mend their lives, change her approach, change herself, get through the rough patch so they could finish their story, their happy lives together, basking in the glow as they grew older, of all their hard work and love, which would make their relationship deeper and stronger, adding depth to their unbreakable bond. The sharp slap in the face that this was only her expectation was devastating. She focused on the part of the windshield where it met the dash board, trying to catch her breath but just hiccupping and gasping, trying to stay as quiet as she could. She really just wanted to open the car door, fall out of the car and lie on the road, howling.

She knew she could not though. She had Noah to think of. She *had* to keep it together—for Noah.

They drove silently through the streets. Gemma doing her best to breathe deeply and calm herself down. Scott was focused on the road. She didn't know what to say, so she said nothing. She didn't trust herself. So many thoughts…how did the night take such a shitty turn? Was it her fault? *No*, she knew it was not. That didn't make her feel any less rejected and let down, however. Hadn't they been having a good time together? She had moments of anger flick through her mind as well. Who did he think he was, playing her like that? He *must* have feelings for Janine. Was it just totally obvious the whole time and she was in denial? She didn't know who to trust. Was it possible someone she knew inside out and back to front was really just a lying scumbag? When he told her about Janine's inappropriate attention, Gemma knew he was telling the truth—or did she? Was it because she wanted to believe? *Does everyone at his work totally know something is going on, and they just avoid me because I look like a dumbass?* No, she had a pretty good intuition when it came to lies and people telling them, and if anything, it was Janine who had always given her the suspicious feelings. The chick that seemed to not have any respect for other people's boundaries. Even when it was spelled out for her to *back off*, still, she plowed forward. Janine was a manipulative, narcissistic piece of work for sure.

Right at that moment, Gemma hated Janine with more hatred than she'd ever felt in her life. She felt it burn at the base of her throat and her vision narrow at the thought of being able to commit some awful act of violence, to let Janine know that she was not to be messed with.

Gemma recognized every conniving, nasty marriage-wrecking bitch she'd ever known all rolled into one ugly package, right there in Janine, and there was no doubting, she had her husband in her sights.

Scott, who had had his share of relationships and affairs before Gemma, was no innocent either. Gemma let out a big sigh—along with it, all desire to hurt anyone. What was unfolding here? She was so conflicted right now.

Was she just being completely taken for a ride? Or were they being totally played by a selfish homewrecker who didn't give two figs about anyone else except for herself?

Dear Lord, please guide me, let me understand the truth, Please walk with Scott, stand by him. She pleaded silently.

She hoped God was listening. She did feel a little bit of peace. Or maybe she just wished she did.

Chapter 15

Physical Pain and Broken Hearts

As they pulled into the driveway, Gemma wiped her eyes, took a deep quivering breath and asked Scott what he was going to do. She couldn't believe she was asking him, but what else was she going to do? What was she supposed to say? Tell him what to do? Lay some sort of guilt trip on him? If he didn't want to be with her, she couldn't very well guilt him into being with her. That would be even worse. The pain of being rejected by her human, her husband, felt physical. She didn't even know if her legs would work when she would need them to get out of the car. She couldn't bring herself to look at him. She didn't want to see the look on his face.

He turned to look at her. "Gem, would you look at me?" he asked softly. The change in his tone and demeanor made her turn to him inquisitively. "Look, I'm sorry. This wasn't how I thought tonight would go."

Gemma caught herself in a half-laugh. "You're telling me!" she answered.

This was definitely *not* how she had thought tonight was going to turn out.

"Look, you're right, there is no reason for me to go over there." Gemma assumed he meant Janine's place. "I'll call her to make sure she's being taken care of, and then how about you and I watch *Forrest Gump* or something and have a night cap?" *Forrest Gump* was their go-to chill-out, feel-good movie and had been for years.

Gemma was caught completely off guard. "Um, okay—I feel like an idiot. I was just really enjoying our night together. It felt like the old you was back, and I really miss you," she offered.

"I know." He took her hand.

"Can you just text her? I'm sure she's got enough of a support system rallying around them without you having to jump in and take responsibility for her emotional state?" she ventured. "If what you say is true about how you feel about her, that would be way more appropriate."

"I suppose," he agreed. He picked up his phone and started texting.

Gemma just stayed in the car, watching him. He sent it and looked at Gemma. She suddenly felt very tired and worn out. All the previous bubbly buzz had left her, and she just felt flat, worn out, and scared. Who was she kidding? She was terrified. She felt completely off, like watching a giant thunder head forming, shooting lightning in all directions and lighting up the interior of the cloud, torn between wanting to take cover and just watching because it was so impressive.

As they got out of the car, Scott's phone rang. Gemma shot him a look. "It's her, isn't it?"

"I'll be quick," he muttered something else as he answered. He gestured for Gemma to go up the stairs toward the front door ahead of him.

Although she wanted to hear what he was going to say to her, Gemma just couldn't. She was a terrible eavesdropper, but she stood at the door, waiting for him. Scott was still on the bottom step. She couldn't really hear what he was saying, but he sounded like he was talking to a close friend. His tone, she totally understood. It wasn't the tone you used with a regular employee. She strained to hear any words, marginally comforted that it wasn't an intimate tone either. She could hear him, repeating, "I'm sorry," but she couldn't quite make out what exactly he was sorry for. Gemma didn't care. Hopefully it was that he was sorry he wasn't going to go running over there to be with her or he was sorry about Daniel's loss. She was so tired. Gemma felt exhausted, like her legs might buckle and as if the ground was heaving underneath her. She felt dizzy and couldn't quite get her breath. Was she having some sort of medical issue?

It dawned on Gemma that she was so thrown off balance because her center was gone. Her rock, her anchor for such a long time, was gone. She felt like she'd been set adrift, floating in an emotional sea of uncertainty, more terrified than she had ever felt before.

Gemma realized she had better re-establish an anchor somewhere, somehow, and quickly. She turned and focused on the doormat, trying to control her breathing.

Scott had finished his phone call and was coming up the stairs toward her. He was looking at her with a strange look on his face. "Are you feeling okay?"

Gemma swallowed hard and managed to shake her head. She could hardly speak. It was like someone was pulling the blinds down as consciousness slipped away from her.

She was aware of Scott lunging forward and grabbing her under her arms.

Oh boy. Gemma fought to keep her eyes open, but it didn't work.

As the darkness gave her tunnel vision and she had a lump in her throat, she let go and lost consciousness.

She figured she was only out for a few seconds, if that. When she reopened her eyes, she was on the floor inside the house, just inside the door. Scott was crouched over her stroking her face, looking like he might cry.

"Oh my god Gemma, are you okay?"

She almost laughed at how concerned he was, but she actually really appreciated it. Somewhere in there, he still cared, right?

"Stay there, I'll get you some water." He leapt up and ran into the kitchen. She heard the cupboard door open and close and the sound of the water dispenser on the fridge. It was an incredibly normal hum that somehow calmed her and bought her back to the room. Everything else was eerily quiet. No AC humming, no radio on, no sounds from outside. Gary came over and walked over her, purring. How undignified. Here she was lying on the floor in the doorway with the cat using her like a doormat. She was aware that in any other moment, she would see the humor in that. But not now.

She started to sit up. "Wait, let me help." Scott fussed as he came back with a glass of water and put one hand behind her propping her up. "What happened? Are you sick? Do you need to go to the emergency room? I'll take you to the hospital. Does anything hurt? I'll take you a doctor."

"I'm okay, I'm fine. I don't know what happened. I'm fine, and besides, I don't have any health insurance, remember?" Scott had forgotten to renew his medical insurance at work, so currently she and Noah were without health insurance. Conveniently, his was auto-renewed. Gemma felt strangely embarrassed and generally upset. She started to cry. Again —big fat tears rolling down her face. She didn't care. Scott patted her awkwardly on the back. This was hopeless.

Gemma cried for a few moments and took a big sniff. There was something pressing on her—a sucky conversation they had to have. She couldn't continue.

Scott got up and fetched some tissues. Without a word, he sat down next to her and put his arm around her. She leaned into him and pulled herself together.

"I'm sorry, honey," he murmured, pushing her hair out of her face. She knew he actually meant it. In this moment, he was being the real Scott.

She sat up straight, and turned to look at him. "What's going on Scott? Are we done?"

He awkwardly looked down. She knew.

"Is there someone else? Is it Janine?"

"No, there's no one else." He paused. "I'm just not in love with you anymore." He kept looking down. "I just don't see us being together any more. I don't want to be a husband any more. You don't like the things that I like. You don't like to do the things that I like to do. I feel like you expect me to do too much, and you make out like you have to do everything, like I am useless. You resent me when I have any type of release with my friends. It's like you don't want me to have any sort of life or friends outside of our marriage. It's not my fault you don't get to hang out with your friends. You should make more of an effort to spend time with them. You just don't like to have fun anymore. Janine's fun to be around, but I'm not fucking her or anything. She gets what it feels like when your marriage isn't working out. I can talk to her. I just don't think I'm cut out to be married, that's all." He looked away awkwardly.

Gemma wondered if he realized what he was saying. "So…" She struggled to make sense of what he said. His words and his posture just didn't line up. "What does that mean? Do you think we're supposed to just be in love forever? Can't we just *love* each other and still be together? Wow, Scott, do you really expect to be in love your whole life? I don't understand. Have you felt like this for the last eighteen years?" She searched his face. Her stomach churned. What was he saying? She didn't believe what she was hearing. It didn't even sound like his words. Or were those his words, and she had just been totally delusional this whole time? What was real? What was she supposed to believe right now? So that was it? Scott wasn't in love anymore so that's the reason to give up on their marriage? How long had he been lying for? Was he lying about him and Janine?

Gemma felt her chest tightening trying to comprehend exactly what this meant. She sat up straighter, suddenly wanting to be away from him. OMG. Was this actually happening? Was this how her marriage would end?

Was he kidding right now? Gemma searched his face for some kind of indicator of…what? Anything to tell her…what?

She was so confused, she felt like her mind was swimming through molasses. She struggled to find something that made sense here.

He leaned forward to put his arm around her. She backed up further. "What are you doing?"

He just told her he wasn't in love with her anymore, and she was supposed to be okay with that? Was he trying to console her?

"Come on, Gem, don't be like that." Like this was the most normal thing in the world, and he just told her that she bought the wrong coffee or something.

"It's just that…I…I could be much better as your friend rather than as your husband."

Gemma looked at him as if seeing him for the first time. She could hear his phone vibrating. *Bet it is Janine*, she thought to herself.

She could see him struggling to not pull it out of his pocket. It stopped. Then started again. Gemma kept looking at him. He looked genuinely conflicted. On the third time, he looked at her, his eyes pleading. Gemma looked away, then looked back, and hissed "Answer it if you feel you have to."

Scott shook his head very slightly, staring at her with wide eyes. Why was he watching her so intently? To see if his words had hit their mark? If she was just going to say, "Okay, cool"? Did he even comprehend what he just said to her?

Gemma felt surreal, like she was disconnected from herself, and it felt like her stomach was pulling her chest down by a lead ball and like her throat was being gripped by a pair of invisible hands.

Was she going to faint again? She couldn't even cry or speak; she could barely breathe.

Gemma got up off the floor and stood there, staring at him, incredulous. Surely he couldn't be serious? Was that it?

He's not in love with me, and we don't have the same interests so that's it? He must be having an affair, that's totally got to be it!

Gemma forced herself to swallow. It felt like a giant rock in her throat.

Still, she could hear his phone buzzing. It would stop and then start again a few moments later. Geez, Gemma knew it was Janine. Holy crap, couldn't she take a freaking hint? Gemma's whole life was ripping apart. Her heart felt like it was in a vice.

She could hear the ice maker in the freezer turning over another batch of ice. She could hear Gary purring on the couch behind her.

Scott still stared at her.

Gemma felt like her whole life was disintegrating, crumbling, and turning to ash right in front of her.

"Who is it? Is it Janine?"

"Who is it, what?" Scott asked.

"Who are you seeing? Are you having sex with someone else?"

"No!" he answered defensively. He tried an incredulous scoff, but it just came out a choked laugh.

"It's Janine, isn't it? Stupid skank can't leave you alone."

"What? *No*, it's not her. She's just been a really good friend, that's all. She's been there for me, and we're having similar issues in our marriages."

"Good grief, Scott! Are you that naive? She's blatantly *grooming* you! There is *nothing* our marriage has in common with hers!" Gemma was surprised at her sudden outburst of anger. She felt like she was burning.

He looked puzzled. Gemma got up, turned away, and went in to the kitchen. She poured herself a glass of water and raised it to her lips. She took half a sip and put it down disgusted. It tasted awful.

She could still barely swallow. She didn't know what was happening to her.

The physical pain was real and intense, like someone was strangling her and pulling out her stomach at the same time, like there was a boulder on her chest pressing all the air out of her, and the knot in her throat wasn't helping anything either.

She concentrated on taking a full breath in. Scott just stood there, helpless as if he didn't fully comprehend what he'd just said to her or what it meant.

And still, his stupid phone was buzzing away.

Everything was so quiet in their house she could hear her heart beating and her bones struggling to hold her upright.

"Well," he ventured, "what do you want me to do?"

"What? Right now?" she asked.

"Do you want me to leave?"

"No. I don't know, Scott. Noah will be home in the morning, what do we tell him? Don't you want to talk about this? Are you just ready to give up on everything? Is that it?" Gemma felt ripped off. "Have you thought this through? What is your plan?"

Scott swallowed hard. No, he hadn't thought it through. Dumb ass.

And still the stupid phone!

"Would you turn your phone off please?" Gemma asked as civilly as she could. *Holy crap, tell the bitch to back up. You just broke your wife's heart wide open, have some respect!* She wanted to scream. But she did not.

Her emotions and temper were all over the place. Gemma did not know how she felt. Was she having a heart attack? She was in so much pain suddenly everywhere.

Gemma paced around the kitchen, not knowing what to do with herself. She didn't know what she wanted to happen.

She didn't want him to go, she didn't want him to stay. She wanted him to hold her, she didn't want him to touch her. She didn't want to be alone, she didn't know who to call, she didn't know what she'd say. Where would he go anyway? Probably to Janine's, his new best friend's house. God, she felt so awful.

He took his phone out of his pocket and turned it off. He put it on the table as he came into the kitchen and looked at her with a semi-concerned look on his face. She tried to push past him, suddenly feeling claustrophobic. He tried to stop her by grabbing her by the shoulders. She made a half-hearted attempt to pull away from him. Suddenly she felt weak, and he turned her to look at him. Gemma could not meet his eyes. He gently lifted her face so that she was looking directly at him.

"I'm sorry, Gemma, I'm so sorry."

She felt the tears coming, like a flashflood raging, burning out of her eyes. She caved with a giant sob, and he pulled her into him. She sobbed like a child leaning on his chest, like her whole world had just been torn away from her—because it had.

Nothing was ever going to be the same between them again. All her visions of growing old together, travelling with Noah, being in a comfortable, stable relationship with one amazing person for the rest of her life were slipping out of her grasp like sand running through her fingers. Everything she had believed, everything she knew, expected and known about their future, gone.

He held her tight for a moment then patted her on the back—one of those "Okay, let's wrap this awkward moment up" pats. *Like the same way you'd pat a stranger*, Gemma thought miserably.

Gemma kept sobbing as she leaned back away from him and slid down the fridge onto the floor.

In the back of her mind, she thought, *I finally get it. All those songs about crying on the kitchen floor. WTF. In another time, it may have even been funny.*

She buried her face in her arms and cried. She cried for her stupidity, that she should have seen this coming. She cried for her sense of betrayal and that she had lost the man she loved so much and held so dear. She cried for the loss of her family. She howled and sobbed till she had no more tears left, and she had had a headache. Eventually she managed to pull herself together. She was still hiccupping as she pushed herself to sit up. She could smell the kitchen rug and hear the ice maker filling up with more water for the next batch. She could hear the tap dripping ever so slowly and the clock on the wall in the living room ticking. She had no idea what time it was. Was it late? Early? It seemed like earlier in the evening had been years ago. Was it even the same night?

She couldn't hear Scott. Had he left? She didn't want to raise her head to find out. She just wanted the whole world to stop, so she could just stay there in a little ball and die.

Chapter 16

Abandoned and Coping

Okay, girlfriend, she pep-talked herself, *you can't stay on the floor all night.* She took a few deep breaths, jagged and hiccupping, but eventually they became more even.

She still felt awful.

Was that her phone ringing?

She wondered where her phone was. When was the last time she even saw it?

It must be in her hand bag. Gemma stood up slowly, feeling stiff and sore. She still had the feeling of a boulder on her chest and like she was being stabbed in the heart with her stomach around her knees.

She took a sip of the water that she had left on the counter. It tasted okay now.

That was her phone ringing, Scott was nowhere in sight.

Noah! Her thoughts turned quickly to her son. She found her phone. It was Sarah, Ryan's mom, the friend he was staying with.

She sounded apologetic. "I'm sorry to bother you so late. I know you were having date night with Scott, but…" She paused as if unsure of what Gemma was going to say or what she was going to say. Gemma's mind raced, suddenly worried about her boy, but didn't say anything, Sarah continued sounding somewhat panicked. "It's just that Ryan and Dylan are both throwing up. Noah is okay, but he really wants to go home. He's upset. I think it's probably for the best. Would you come and pick him up?" In the background, she could hear water running and the sounds of general mayhem—one child heaving, another woeful "Mom..." *What time was it?* Gemma wondered again.

"Oh no! That's awful! Of course, I'll come get him!" Gemma replied, surprised at hearing her voice sound relatively normal. "Are the boys okay? Are you okay? Is it a bug or something they ate? Can I pick you up anything on the way over?" They lived about ten minutes away, but Gemma knew she passed a twenty-four-hour supermarket on the way. Gemma was surprised at her sudden coherent ability.

Sarah sounded exhausted. "We're okay. I don't think I need anything. I'm fine except for being surrounded by vomit." She gave a half-hearted laugh. "I think it was the leftover barbeque they had for lunch at their grandmother's. She's notorious for keeping food longer than she should and then feeding it to her family!" Gemma could hear irritation in Sarah's voice. She remembered they had laughed about her mother-in-law's fridge before, but it wasn't so funny now.

"No problem, Sarah. I'll be there in about fifteen minutes."

"Thank you." Sarah sounded like she might cry with relief.

Gemma ended the call and looked at the time. 11:15 p.m., was that it? It felt like Gemma had dropped him off at Sarah's days ago, not just that afternoon.

Gemma walked down the hallway to her bedroom. She thought maybe she should get changed out of the dress she put on so long ago with so much anticipation. Where was Scott? *Probably at Janine's. Jerk*, she thought halfheartedly. What was she going to do now?

No time for those thoughts. She had to put on her mom-face and deal with it.

The house was very still and very quiet. She checked herself in the mirror. Not too much of a train wreck, a little wrinkled, and puffy-eyed, but she could just say she fell asleep on the couch or something. She doubted Sarah would even notice being that she had her own drama to deal with right now. She splashed some water on her face, repinned her hair, and grabbed her purse as she headed out the door while rummaging for lip gloss and some gum.

The most important thing was getting Noah. Poor guy, poor Sarah, poor Ryan and Dylan. She knew Noah and Ryan had been so excited about the sleepover, just as she had begun the night with so much excitement and anticipation. Turned out to be a terrible night for everyone. Gemma took another big hiccup-y breath in as she popped some gum in her mouth and got into her car.

She noticed Scott's car was not in the driveway, but it didn't really register.

Her main concern right now was bringing Noah home. Hopefully he wouldn't pick up whatever the boys had. Gemma pulled out of the driveway and drove up to the corner past Janine's house. Scott's car wasn't in the driveway there either, but it looked like every light in the house was on. She had a momentary pang of sorrow for Daniel's family and Daniel. She said a silent prayer for them all.

As Gemma drove through the dark streets, the sky was clear. She could see so many stars. Against the dark and velvety sky, there was a tiny sliver of new moon hanging low in the sky. Everything looked different, but she realized with a pang, it was just her that was different. Gemma found herself trying hard to focus on being a good mom, wondering if Noah was okay, hoping again he didn't end up with some vomit-y bug, pushing away any conflicting feelings of hurt and anger.

She started speaking a prayer.

Lord, if you're listening right now, I could really do with some direction here or peace or closure or something. She ran out of words, not even sure what to say or what she was asking for. The streets were quiet, and she got every green light. She pulled into Sarah's driveway in no time.

Sarah met her at the door with Noah and his backpack and his pillow. She looked worn out. Gemma could smell the piney scent of disinfectant and household cleaner.

Noah lunged at Gemma, wrapping his arms tightly around her waist. "Mom!" Gemma hugged him back. Sarah apologized to Gemma and Noah. Gemma reassured her that everything was fine. They could absolutely do it another night. Sarah didn't ask about the date night, and Gemma didn't offer.

They headed back to the car, and Noah climbed into the backseat. As soon as they were both in the car, Noah started talking. "Mom, I'm so glad to see you! It was so gross!" Noah said, excited to share the terrible tale. "We were playing that race car game on their PlayStation, then Ryan said he didn't feel very good, he turned a strange white and green color and just started hurling. He vomited all over himself, and then it spurted out of his hands cause he was trying to keep it in, and he left a vomit trail all the way down the hall to the bathroom. Then Dylan started laughing and their mom was freaking out and trying to get a bucket and the dog was trying lick the carpet and then Dylan said he didn't feel very good and then *he* vomited too! But he made it to the kitchen sink! Mom, it was so gross and smelt horrible, and Dylan was still kind of laughing, but then he started crying and I didn't know if he was laughing or crying and their mom was trying to yell upstairs to their dad, but he wasn't answering." Noah paused for a breath.

"Wow," said Gemma, "Sounds messy."

"And stinky, Mom. It smelt so bad." He paused. "Can you turn on the radio? It's really quiet in here." Gemma smiled to herself, amused that in the middle of his story he noticed that the radio was not on.

"So you said the dog was licking the floor?"

"Oh yes, it was so gross, and then when Ryan's dad did come downstairs and saw and smelt what was happening, he started doing that thing that dad does." Noah made the heaving dry retching sound that men make. He started laughing. Gemma laughed too in spite of herself.

"Good grief, it sounds awful."

"Oh, Mom, it was." Noah yawned. "Can you make me some of your amazing hot chocolate when we get home, and can I sleep in your bed?" he asked hopefully.

Gemma smiled into the rear vision mirror. "Of course honey," The hot chocolate he loved so much was so amazing to him because she added vanilla almond creamer to it. He loved it.

Noah was barely visible except for random patches of streetlights they drove through like pools in the darkness. She could see him smile as he put his head on his pillow which he had propped up against the side of his seatbelt. "Thanks, Mom, that'll be great. It's late, isn't it?" he trailed off.

"Yes, honey, it's very late." Gemma looked in the rear vision mirror again at the lights. He was asleep, looking like the sweet angel he was.

Gemma had no idea what was going to happen now, who could she talk to? Scott had been the person she turned to or leaned on whenever she was in doubt. OMG, who now? She couldn't fall apart. She had to keep it together for Noah, had to keep her head up, had to get out away from here. She could get through this. She had to keep going for him. And for herself. They were all each other had. That thought made her feel sad, momentarily wishing she had a family member or even a close friend she could turn to. She didn't feel close enough to Celia to dump all this on her. She felt grateful she could still talk to God; she knew she was never really alone.

The car hummed softly as she waited for the light to change. The song on the radio was starting, suddenly becoming incredibly valid to her current situation, like a message from heaven.

"You call me out upon the waters/the great unknown, where feet may fail/And there I find you in the mystery, in oceans deep/my faith will stand/and I will call upon your name."

It had been one of her favorites for a while, but tonight in the car, with her wonderful love affair all undone and over, her precious little boy sleeping soundly in the back seat, feeling like she was lost and crushed and drowning, it took on a whole new meaning, like it was written just for her and her situation, letting her know that God was there, reassuring and validating at the same time. The tears started streaming down her cheeks but different tears this time—silent, grief-filled, heartbreaking tears of acceptance and resignation.

She started singing along her voice trembling and choked. "And keep my eyes above the waves/When oceans rise, my soul will rest in Your embrace/For I am Yours and You are mine/Your grace abounds in deepest waters/Your sovereign hand/Will be my guide/Where feet may fail and fear surrounds me/You've never failed and you won't start now/So I will call upon your name/And keep my eyes above the waves/When oceans rise, my soul will rest in your embrace/For I am yours and you are mine/Spirit lead me where my trust is without borders/Let me walk upon your waters/Where ever you would call me/Take me deeper than my feet could ever wander/And my faith will be made stronger/In the presence on my Savior."

Gemma pulled into the driveway and saw Scott's car there. She turned off the engine and took a few deep breaths as she sat and listened to the end of the song.

Time to get her little man in the house. Game face on…oh, who was she kidding? She didn't even care.

She twisted in her seat and gently shook Noah. "Honey, wake up," she said softly. "We're home." Noah barely stirred. "Honey." Gemma was a little louder. "Noah, wake up, we're home."

Still nothing. Gemma sat there, looking at him while he slept, weighing up whether or not she could still carry him. At almost nine years old, he wasn't the skinniest kid on the block, but he wasn't particularly hefty either. She knew she could still piggyback him, but a sleepy deadweight, she doubted her ability to wrangle him out gently, and besides, she was not feeling very strong.

In fact, this whole night she had been feeling decidedly weak and unable to trust her body. Fainting on the floor had been fairly alarming. She had only fainted twice before in her whole life.

She didn't want to go in and see if Scott was there to help, but she did want to go in and see if he was there.

She wanted him to say he was wrong and so very sorry and would she take him back and could he ever make it up to her.

Gemma almost laughed at the sheer lunacy of *that* idea. As if. And then she felt like crying again.

All those times that she had silently scoffed at women who held a flame for the men who had "done them wrong," and here she was doing the same thing. She was aware of how raw and wounded she felt, like a mess, all over the place, and she was so tired and weary. Everything ached.

Surely Scott was just having "a moment." He couldn't be serious.

She knew in her soul he was very serious though. It explained everything and his distance from her, the way he had pulled away further and further over the last few months. How she had been making excuses for his distance, when really, everything had been staring her in the face—she had been so stupid.

Gemma couldn't help it. She started crying again. Geez, where are all these tears coming from?

Again, she momentarily returned to the thought that she should have known that someone who had made her feel so loved and secure would have the potential to make her feel just as unloved and insecure too.

Gemma put her head in her hands and leaned against the steering wheel. From the back, she heard Noah's sleepy voice: "Mom? Mom? Are you crying? Are you okay?"

Gemma sat up and took a halting breath in, wiping away the tears. "Yes, honey, I'm okay, just feeling a bit sad, but hey, we're home," she said changing the subject. "How about that hot chocolate and sleep in my bed special?"

"Mmm, yes, that would be good," he murmured. Gemma got out of the car and opened his door for him. He climbed out with his pillow. She put her arm around him as he leaned in for a quick hug. "Would you get my bag, Mom?"

"Of course."

He waited for her. "I'm sorry you had to come and pick me up."

"Oh, Noah! I'm not sorry, I will always, always come and bring you home when you need me!"

"Did you have a fight with Dad?" he asked, his big brown eyes looking up to her.

"Not really." She didn't know what else to say right now. She had never lied to him, but she was aware of overwhelming him too. What the hell was she going to say anyway? *Daddy isn't in love with me anymore and doesn't want to be my husband because he has a major freaking flaw that I had completely overlooked where he thinks he's supposed to be in love forever? Or Daddy would rather hang out with a bunch of cool kids he works with, especially the one crappy human being who lives right across the street?*

WTF. Gemma sighed. No, she couldn't tell him that. She'd have to process this herself first. "Let's get that hot chocolate!" She steered him toward the stairs as she closed the car door.

As they entered the house, Gemma could smell alcohol. Scott was passed out on the couch with a bottle of Fireball on the coffee table and a shot glass in his hand. She was not surprised at all.

Noah was distracted by Gary, who was on the kitchen counter. Gemma took the opportunity to guide him down the hallway. He didn't even glance at the couch.

"Come on, buddy, how about you warm up the bed for me, and I'll bring you your hot chocolate?"

"Can I watch TV too?" Noah asked hopefully.

"Sure, honey." She mussed up his hair. It didn't really matter right now. Whether or not Noah was watching television at midnight seemed like a very insignificant thing for her to be worrying about.

She tucked him into bed, turned on the TV for him, and found something appropriate for him to watch. She was mildly surprised that were so many kid-friendly options around midnight and went back down the hall to make his hot chocolate. Gemma was surprised to see Scott sitting up when she got back to the kitchen. He was upright on the couch, his eyes glazed and blurry-looking. He looked completely wasted.

"Where did you go?" he asked. "I was worried."

Gemma nearly laughed out loud. Seriously, what did he care she went? *Mr. I'll-just-drive-off-and-don't-give-a-rat's-ass-about-how-you-feel-about-it, but oh no, where did YOU go?*

He stood up, a little unsteady, and asked her again. "Where were you?"

Gemma didn't look at him. Did he even remember what he'd told her earlier?

"Sarah called and asked me to go and get Noah cause Ryan and Dylan came down with a tummy bug." She paused a moment. Scott said nothing. "So I did." Still nothing.

He sat back down. "Shit, okay."

Gemma shot him a sideways look. *Well, that was a weird reply.* "But yes, Noah is fine," she added sarcastically.

"I was going to ask, you just didn't give me a chance," he snapped.

"Okay, whatever." At this point, she didn't care. She was beyond exhausted, worn down, and weary after her seemingly endless night that started so full of light and hope and joy. Gemma felt like she had been on a rollercoaster. She didn't give a crap about how Scott felt about her reply or whether his feelings were hurt or anything really,

Gemma finished making Noah's hot chocolate, turned, and walked back down the hallway toward her bedroom. Noah was sound asleep diagonally across the bed. Gary was on one of the pillows purring loudly.

Gemma stood there for a moment, watching them sleep so peacefully. She sat on the edge of the bed and drank the hot chocolate herself. It was warm and soothing.

What am I going to do now? she pondered sadly to herself, feeling the empty void of an abandoned woman.

She changed out of her dress and left it in a pile on the floor. Who cares? She put on her pajamas, kneeled next to the bed like she used when she was a child, hung her head, and prayed—The most honest vulnerable prayer she'd ever prayed in her life.

Lord, I am lost, alone, abandoned, and broken. Please guide me gently. Light my way. I am nothing, I have nothing. I surrender. Let your will overtake my heart and my life. Guide me, Lord. Keep me safe. Give me strength to keep going and shelter my child. Guide us. Let me keep it together for my son.

Tears were streaming down her face again. She made the sign of the cross.

Amen.

Gemma climbed into bed somewhere between Noah and Gary and tried to sleep. She lay there for a long time with her eyes closed. Not quite asleep, not quite awake. Feeling empty and resigned, wondering where she would go and what she would do to take care of Noah and Gary, she eventually fell into a fitful sleep.

Chapter 17

Kintsugi—Golden Joinery

During the night, Gemma woke up slowly, unsure of where she was. She felt very serene and at peace. It was dark, and she was aware of a bright golden light shining very close to her. As she sat up, she realized it was coming from her. There was a bright seam that looked like the Japanese pottery that they repair with gold, right through her middle reaching around her sides. It was so brilliant and golden white that she could not look at herself, glorious and shining, golden, illuminating the room. Gemma felt very peaceful and calm. She knew everything was going to be all right. She no longer felt upset and torn, she was serene and secure.

She knew God was with her.

Gemma laid back down and went back to sleep.

In the morning, she woke up quietly coming to awareness. She realized she must have only been asleep for five or so hours. She was awake. As she lay there, listening to the sounds in her house and outside, she knew it must still be very early. Listening to Noah breathing was the only sound she could really hear and the breeze outside in the big tree outside her window.

She had no idea what time it was but knew she had to go to the toilet. *Ugh. Who needs an alarm when you have a bladder?*

Gary was sitting at the end of the bed, staring at her with his green eyes, his tail making lazy sweeping motions. She could hear him purring as she got out of bed. Everything was so peaceful in her room. Gemma went to the bathroom and looked in the mirror. She almost laughed at the sad-eyed raccoon face staring back at her. Or was it more goth-inspired? Her eyes were red-rimmed. She couldn't tell if it was from crying so much last night or sleeping with all of her make up on. Mascara wasn't exactly recommended as a nighttime sleep addition. She really should have washed her face before bed.

As she ran the faucet, she inspected her face. Wow, emotional trauma will really age a person. Although she knew crying your eyes out for hours and sleeping in a full face of makeup doesn't help in the short term either. As she took off her eye makeup, she looked at herself with compassion and was surprised to still feel very serene. Was that a dream she had in the night? She was fairly certain it really happened, didn't it? She did still feel the overwhelming peace on a level she hadn't felt previously. Well, peace was the predominant feeling. Is that what people mean when they say they were "touched by the Lord"? She was pretty sure that was what had happened but felt just as sure this was something she wasn't comfortable telling anyone about—yet, anyway.

Terrified and unsure of what was to come or how to verbalize what had happened during the night, she was ultimately peaceful with it.

Gemma knew God was with her, and if she could just trust in the process, his process, and not let the undercurrent of fear over take her, she would be okay. Simple. She continued to stare into her own eyes and let out a long sigh. Again.

It was controlling that undercurrent of fear that would need work.

She tried to reason out the whole situation in her mind.

Surely Scott was wrong. He was just being a typical aging man, acting the fool, blinded by his own alcohol-fueled, ego-driven ideas of ease, that he was just infatuated with Janine. Her barbie doll looks, stupid bimbo face, and big eyes that looked at him with such manipulative adoration, as well as her scanty clothing was all very head-turning for a forty-plus-year-old married man suddenly mired in the reality of life, who was always looking for the next party, someone to drink with. Turned out he wasn't viewing the progression of their union quite like she was. Gemma had always thought of their relationship like a garden—a fantastic work in progress that they had spent time digging and weeding and watering and planting, both working hard on their life together and getting closer to harvest, secure in the knowledge that they were in it together for the long haul. Well, she viewed it that way—by herself, obviously. She wondered how much other stuff she had naturally presumed about their lives together was totally wrong. But this was stuff that they had talked about, agreed upon!

What a rude awakening. Gemma felt tears welling up, still surprised at the way her emotions flashed through her with so much force and power.

He had just been looking for the next best thing—the whole damn time?!

Ouch. Was it possible she had been completely delusional for the last eighteen years?

Apparently so. Again, ouch.

Gemma sighed again, brushed away the tears, and turned on the shower. She could not let herself go down *that* path of thinking, as it would surely lead to nowhere good. It was just fear raising its ugly head. Right now, she needed to be building herself up, supporting herself, not tearing herself down with insecure inadequacies. Or if she wasn't quite there yet, at least be gentle with herself.

She rummaged through the bathroom cupboard for one of her favorite body washes. Also finding a rose face mask and a half full tub of body butter she had been given for Christmas, that was a pleasant surprise. She had forgotten all about it. It was a heavenly green ivy and lavender scent. Gemma took the lid off and let the aroma waft around the bathroom, mingling with the humidity from the shower. She smeared the face mask on and took one solid deep breath, feeling a little more grounded as she got into the shower.

The hot water felt good, and she stood there for a while, barely moving, letting the water run down her head, face and body. She wished she could dissolve and run down the plug hole away from everything, away from what lay ahead of her, what she had to deal with now.

That weight was still pressing on her, making it hard to breathe. Fear kicked in again.

Holy crap, does everyone know? Is this one of those the-wife-is-the-last-to-know things? Has he been telling people his marriage was over for months while I've been working on fixing it this whole time? Is he lying to me? What else is he lying about? Has everything in our lives so far been a lie? Is he having sex with someone else? Gemma felt unnerved that the person she had trusted the most for the longest time was obviously so untrustworthy. This was a hugely disturbing feeling all on its own. *Has he been lying to me this whole time? Has he?* Good grief. She felt like all the air had been sucked out of her. *If he's been lying about this, what else was he lying about?*

"Mom?" she heard Noah knocking on the bathroom door.

Gemma snapped back to reality. She could hear him talking but could not hear the words he was saying. "Come in, honey," she called.

Noah opened the door. She wasn't concerned, there was a shower curtain between them. 'Mom, I'm hungry. Can we have breakfast?"

"Sure, Noah, go get yourself a glass of water and a banana and turn on the TV. I'll be out in a minute."

"Okay." The door closed again.

Gemma finished up in the shower, taking her time, pep-talking herself. She felt awful.

She caught herself in the mirror. Gone was the happy look in her eyes she knew so well. She looked hollow, dull and empty.

Gemma put on her clothes and some mascara and lip gloss. She pulled back her hair into a loose ponytail. With a sigh, she headed out of the bathroom in the direction of the kitchen.

She could hear the TV on in the living room but nothing else.

She guessed Scott was not home, but caught herself wondering if he was there passed out on the couch? She wondered what his next move would be. She aimlessly walked into the kitchen, not even feeling like her feet were on the ground.

What should she do? Kick him out? No, she didn't want to do that. Demand they return to counselling? Make him go to AA? Why?

Gemma felt unsteady and lost. She momentarily thought about calling a member of her family, but who? The thought of having to explain everything to someone was tiring. No, she'd have to deal with this on her own.

Gemma pulled out the toaster, some eggs and a frying pan automatically.

"Mom, can we have dipping eggs?" Noah asked hopefully, his innocent happy face popping up at the edge of the counter.

"Sure, babe." She smiled at him. Noah had called them dipping eggs since he could speak, his absolute favorite—fried and just runny enough to dip his toast into.

"What's wrong, Mom? You have your sad face on."

"I'm okay, honey, just thinking about things, and I'm tired." Gemma kicked herself for using the lame old standby—tired—but it was the truth. She was more exhausted than she had ever been in her whole entire life. Her body, mind, heart, and soul felt fatigued.

Gary jumped up onto the counter, pushing his head into Noah's.

Noah stood there a moment longer, letting Gary use him as a rubbing post. "I closed Dad's door. He was snoring really loudly, and I couldn't hear the TV."

Gemma's heart jumped a little—or was that lurched? So he was at home.

She fought the urge to go to his room and ask him: Why? Why didn't he want her anymore? Why did he think they had to be in love forever? Was everything he said a lie? *Has most of the last twenty years of my life been a giant delusion?*

Then she remembered her dream and felt a sense of peace overcome her. She took a deep, shaky breath in and let it out in a sigh. Another breath in, a bit more sure this time.

It was okay, she had this. She turned the radio on in the kitchen and found the worship station they had been listening to in the car. The music helped her feel even more peace.

Noah came over and gave her a big waist hug. "Mom!" he exclaimed, looking up adoringly. "I can reach all the way around you! I can almost hold my own hands!"

Gemma laughed in spite of herself. She held his face in her hands and kissed him on the forehead. "Wow, Noah, almost there! You're growing up so fast!"

"Soon I'll be taller than you, right. Mom?"

"Yes, honey, in no time at all." She mussed up his hair and watched him with fondness as he walked back into the living room.

Gemma finished making their breakfast and they sat at the table to eat. She wasn't surprised that the food felt like cardboard in her mouth. She was not hungry at all, she just pushed the food around for a few minutes and then got up from the table. Noah was happily chatting away about what had happened on the cartoon he had just watched. Gemma was really trying to keep up, but she just couldn't. She kept looking around the living area—at the book shelf, the coffee table, the counter—looking at everything. There was just so much stuff! She felt claustrophobic, and started thinking of everything she wanted to throw out and give away. She would get started right after breakfast. She didn't know what was going to happen now, but she had a strong desire to lighten her load, so that she would be ready for whatever was next.

After breakfast, Gemma headed to the garage to see if they had some boxes in there. She found a roll of black trash bags and three boxes. *Well,* she thought to herself, *it's a start.*

Noah was riding his scooter up and down the driveway while Gary sat at the top of the stairs in the sunshine. Everything seemed so normal. Gemma was almost lulled into a false sense of security. She imagined she could probably go back inside and carry on as if it was a normal weekend morning. She was sure Scott would wake up, come out for his coffee, stare at his phone, and everything would just carry on as normal.

But everything was not normal. Everything was falling apart. Her husband, her human, the best friend she'd ever had, didn't want her anymore, and she was no longer his queen or his treasure. The feeling of loss and disparity of suddenly being out in the cold was hard to bear. She had been unceremoniously demoted to something less than…what? Gemma still felt like she had a boulder on her chest. Every breath was a struggle. She couldn't believe the physical pain she felt.

Although she felt squashed and fractured, she also felt a twinge of deep stillness, almost peace. At least now, there was a direction to take. It was time to dissolve whatever was left of her marriage. It was time to face the facts—that Scott did not want to be her husband anymore and he did not want to be with her, time to realize, that everything she had imagined for their lives, no, *her life*, would not be working out that way. She felt foolish like she had just realized she had put all her money on the wrong horse. Now almost twenty years had passed, gone so fast, she had not pursued her own career. She had followed her heart and her man, and now she would have to start over.

She also felt a rising surge of panic. *What was she doing? Where would she go? What would happen to her and Noah and Gary? Where would they live? How would she make enough money to get by?*

She understood in that moment why so many women stick in horrible marriages and relationships—simply because they are too terrified of what may be in store for the future. Better the devil you know, than the devil you don't know. Right? That was not right for Gemma. She could not bear to think the relationship that she had shared with Scott, would now be washed-out, diluted dying embers for the rest of her life. No, it just had to end. He didn't want to be with her, he said so himself, and she knew he was right.

She took a few deep breaths and managed to quell the panic to an uncomfortable anxious feeling.

She figured she would have to get used to that feeling. She didn't see how it would be going away anytime soon. There was so much work ahead of her, so much she had to get through before she would be on the other side of all this.

In that moment, she just felt weary. And empty. And pained. And like she'd lost the most important part of herself. How could all this even be possible?

Gemma heard Noah chatting inside. She hadn't even noticed he'd gone in ahead of her.

Her stomach lurched again. *Dear Lord, that meant Scott was up.* She contemplated getting in the car and driving away for a moment.

But where would she go? That got her. She felt her eyes welling up with tears again.

Wow, I'm a mess. She realized she had run the gamut of huge emotions in mere hours. OMG, she had never experienced anything like this before. Ever.

Never would she have ever imagined that Scott would make her feel this way. Although, she reminded herself again, she should have known, that someone with the capability to make her feel so amazing and incredible and uplifted would also have the capability to make her feel the exact opposite. Well, that reality sucked.

Gemma took a deep breath, folded the two boxes so they would fit into the third box, and headed up the stairs. The front door was open. She could hear Noah talking to Scott in the kitchen. Well, she could hear Noah talking, she didn't hear Scott. She imagined he was probably hungover as hell—his usual weekend MO.

Gemma put the boxes down just inside the front door. She pushed them toward the wall so they would not be in the way.

"—and so dead, you know what?" She could hear Noah, telling him about his latest obsession with all things Nerf. "When you take the Nerf rival, people can actually change them and modify them. It's called modding."

Gemma smiled to herself. His main thing was Nerf guns and "modding" them at the moment. Mainly, she presumed because his friend Ryan had a cousin who did it all of the time. Although she had been wary in the beginning of this older kid trading Nerf guns with Noah, because he was so trusting, it turned out that he was actually a pretty good kid and was hooking Noah up with the different Nerf guns that he had altered in some way or another.

The lack of Scott's response pissed her off—as usual he was totally ignoring him. Why didn't he realize, that he only had such a short window of time that Noah was trying to hold his attention? Why didn't Scott realize, that in no time at all Noah would want nothing to do with him? Scott was such a fool for being a half-hearted Dad. Cat Stevens was onto something with his "Cat's in the Cradle" song.

Okay. She steeled herself. *Time to face him.*

Gemma walked into the kitchen, forcing her legs to keep moving. She plastered a half-smile on her face. "Good morning," she said. She had no idea how it sounded.

Scott turned to face her. For the first time, she saw him as maybe somebody else would. In fact, she almost didn't recognize him. He was just a regular guy. Any previous rose-colored glasses she had worn while looking at him were most definitely off.

Here was Scott—early forties, fairly attractive, obviously worked out and drank too much kind of guy. He looked rough and hungover. He looked like a kid, a college kid who'd had a big night and knew he'd been part of something stupid but didn't know exactly what.

He could hardly meet her eyes. "Look, Gemma, I'm sorry about last night." He looked down at the counter and swallowed hard, or was that trying to not vomit?

"What exactly are you sorry for?" She trailed off. Was he sorry for just how badly the night had ended? Or breaking her heart? Or him admitting he had feelings for Janine? Or what exactly? Gemma looked at him. She could feel the disgust in her gaze.

He flinched. "Don't look at me like that," he said defensively, which automatically pissed her off.

"Like what?" She wanted to yell at him. *Like you broke my heart? Like you just dropped a bomb on my life?* She wanted to scream in his face. But she didn't.

"I think you should move out for a while, Scott. I need some space to deal with all of this." Of course, just then Noah came into the kitchen.

"No!" he yelled, running over to his dad. "You can't move out, Dad!"

Scott looked down at him and put one hand on his head, ruffling his hair. "Don't worry, sport, I'm not going anywhere. Mommy is just"—he paused—"being emotional."

Noah looked at Gemma, for reassurance.

"Come on, son, I'll make you some pop tarts." He guided Noah back into the kitchen and gave Gemma a look as if she had done something wrong.

This was too much for Gemma. She spun on her heel and grabbed her keys. *Was he serious? How dare he act as if he had done nothing wrong and it was all her fault!*

"Where are you going?" Scott asked.

"Out!" she yelled, suddenly losing her composure.

"Where's out?"

"Not in!" Gemma slammed the door, ran down the stairs, and got in her car. She slammed it into reverse and sped out of the driveway.

Chapter 18

Heavenly Intervention

It wasn't until she got to the road that she realized she didn't have anywhere to go. She felt sick when she saw Janine's house and all the cars in their driveway. She had forgotten about the tragedy that had happened to Daniel not even twenty-four hours before.

She headed down the street in the opposite direction as she started crying again. This time, the tears were big fat hot tears filling her eyes and rolling down her cheeks like a burning stream. She could hardly see. Gemma pulled into the back parking lot of a supermarket and howled giant sobs, tears pouring from her eyes, streaming down her face, hiccupping and spluttering. She let it all out. Was she losing her mind? Why didn't Scott take anything she was saying or feeling seriously? Had he been lying to her this whole time? *Oh, Lord, have I been completely delusional thinking I had this great relationship when in actual fact he's been a d-bag the whole time?* Was he having emotional affairs with workmates this whole time? Did everyone he worked with think she was a giant idiot? Did they feel sorry for her? Did they even care? Gemma buried her head in her hands. *NO.* That answer was the most definite thing she had felt in days.

Strangely, she felt the newly familiar sense of peace come over her. She had not been delusional. He had been present, and they *had* enjoyed a great relationship, although again, *had* was the operative word in that sentence. Whatever they had shared was gone, whether or not she was ready to admit it or let it go. And that was what sucked. She took a deep shuddery breath, blew her nose, and pulled herself together. She knew she had to pull herself together for Noah. As his mom, it was up to her to provide him with a sense of security, with or without Scott. She owed it to herself and her son to provide a stable environment for them both. Right then she felt her focus shift.

She drove around town for a while, thinking about everything. What a mess.

Wow, God, am I supposed to be simmering or frying here?

She again felt like she had been simmering for a while. Except now, all the liquid had evaporated, and she was burning a dry pot.

Could God have three or four frying pans for you at once? She knew it must all tie in together but could not see it.

Gemma thought of the story about how to cook a frog. Put it in the water of the pot while cold and turn the heat up very slowly. Before the frog knows to jump out, it's boiled alive.

Although she felt like she was being crushed, not boiled, she did feel like she had ended up sitting in boiling water and had not taken enough notice to jump out. Where would she have jumped anyway? She took a deep breath, trying to quell the crushing feelings. She reconnected with the tenuous peace she knew was in there.

After driving around for a while, she found herself in the parking lot of everyone's favorite megastore.

Gemma sat for a while, watching people—families getting in and out of their cars, walking across the parking lot, normal people going about their normal lives.

Not her. Gemma didn't think she'd ever be normal again. She didn't even know what normal was anymore. She was different, the blinkers were off. There would have to be a new normal. It was not what she was watching. Not this.

"Lord, if you're listening...," Gemma started whispering to herself. She stopped and let out a big sigh. She knew He was listening. He was always listening. "Lord, I'm scared. I don't know what to do. Where am I going to go? What about Noah? And Gary?" She could feel her breath getting quicker, starting to panic.

Okay, Gemma. She took a long breath in. *What do I want from Him?*

She let her breath out in a controlled sigh. So much had happened in the last twenty-four hours. She still felt crushed. Was her marriage over? That was an overwhelming, suffocating thought, but she remembered the peace of her vision. It had felt so real—because it was real. No more questioning and doubting herself.

Gemma leaned back and let that feeling in. That felt good. She sat up straighter and changed her tone. She felt more grounded. Whatever was going to happen now would happen regardless. Heaven had a plan for her. All she had to do was let it unfold. She gave a half-hearted laugh. Sounded easy enough.

Is this what people meant when they said things like "Surrender to the Lord" or "Turn your troubles over to Him"? She liked the sound of that, but never really understood exactly what it meant—*or how to do it.*

Lord, I know you can hear me, she continued. *Please show me a sign. Show me the way to go. I surrender to your will, I accept your path for me.*

She made the sign of the cross and grinned to herself. The Catholic childhood traditions were in ground.

Gemma felt compelled to go inside and walk anonymously around the giant store.

She wandered past the food aisles, pushing a cart drifting aimlessly through the shoe section and turned the corner to the sports department, wondering if she should call Scott, if Noah was okay. *No*, she told herself firmly. *I can be apart from the both of them for a couple of hours. I don't need to be there.*

She thought she heard someone say her name and stopped. After all, Gemma wasn't exactly a common name. She turned around, and walking toward her, she saw Pamela, the older lady who worked with her at the department store, who had originally told her about the community church. Gemma had never been so happy to see someone neutral. Pamela was a friendly lady with sparkly eyes and a smile never too far away from her kind face.

As she walked closer to her, Pamela's face changed to a look of concern. "Are you all right?" Pamela hugged her. Gemma hugged her back relieved to see her. The two women looked at each other, the older one silent.

"Oh Pamela, I've had a tough night and morning." She looked down at the floor, unsure of how to go on but knowing she could not pretend things were okay. "Scott and I are not…" Gemma trailed off, looking down.

Pamela nodded, holding her hand. "Oh, honey, I'm sorry. Do you need a break?" It was Gemma's turn to nod. Pamela had known of Scott's change in behavior and fondness of drinking. The women had chatted together often, sharing the break room at the same time and in quiet moments at work. Pamela had spent her marriage with an alcoholic who had left her with two little kids, nearly twenty-five years ago. Gemma had always admired her strength and compassion. Pamela was the most unassuming, kindest, smartest, best Christian lady she knew, and she loved her story of overcoming such hardship by placing her faith in the Lord and gaining her strength from him. Gemma had even shared the idea of God using everyone as frying pans, training us all to adapt to the ingredients and adjust the heat accordingly. Pamela had given that a lot of thought, and it had been a popular topic of discussion at various times the last few months.

Gemma had been continually amazed at how peaceful and accepting Pamela was of all people and situations she came across. They had also spent a lot of time talking about people triumphing in the face of hardship. Gemma always felt so uplifted after being around her.

She almost cried with relief but kept herself together, simply because she felt it would be inappropriate to burst into tears in the middle of the store full of normal people doing normal weekend activities.

Yet Gemma was sure God had put Pamela in front of her right at this moment.

"Yes." She nodded again. Her eyes filling with tears which she rapidly blinked away. "I could do with a break."

Pamela nodded back. "Well, my dear, I actually need some help." Gemma wondered how she could possibly help anyone at this moment. Pamela continued, "I am going away for two weeks and really need someone reliable to look after my house and my cat. I had a neighbor lined up, but she literally just called this morning to let me know she wouldn't be able to help after all." Pamela sighed. "If you would be able to feed the cat and check on the house, I would appreciate it, you could even stay at the house. The cat's name is Pickles. She's old and sleeps a lot. You could stay for a night or two, or stop by every day, or stay the whole time, it's up to you." Pamela's face was kind, understanding, and hopeful all at the same time. "You would be really helping me out. I've been planning this trip for months, and the kennel has no room for an elderly cat. I fly out tomorrow night…" It was Pamela's turn to trail off.

Gemma felt a ray of hope sweep through her but also a little overwhelmed. "Yes," she heard herself say, "that would be great," barely remembering the trip to Europe Pamela had been excitedly planning and talking about for months.

Pamela stepped back and rummaged in her bag. "Here, I'll give you my address. Can you come over this afternoon? Or in the morning? I need to leave for the airport by 1:00 p.m." She pulled out a mini sticky note pad and pen and wrote a quick a note. After confirming Gemma's number, she sent her a text with the door code.

Pamela smiled at her, a sympathetic smile. "I know it doesn't seem like it right now"—she placed her hand on her arm—"but God does have a plan for you."

Gemma wanted to believe her, she really did. But that was as far as her thoughts would allow her to go.

"What are you doing now?" Pamela asked. "I am heading home soon if you want to come by. I can show you everything? Do you need someone to listen? I could make lunch. Are you hungry?"

Gemma smiled at her. "That would be great, Pamela. I would appreciate it. I would love to help you out. I don't know if I'm ready to talk…still processing everything that's happened in the last day or so." She blinked back tears again and swallowed the giant lump in her throat. She took a deep breath and blew it out, regaining her composure. "I would love to come by and check it all out. I'm not really doing anything right now." She almost felt like Pamela was just having sympathy for her.

Pamela picked up on those thoughts and shook her head. "Gemma, you would really be helping me out here. I think God puts people in front of us for a reason, and I'm sure you could use a change of perspective."

Gemma smiled at her, feeling like the sun had just peeked out from behind the clouds on a rainy day.

"Yes." Gemma nodded, feeling suddenly hopeful again. "You're right, let me finish up here, and I'll head over."

"Wonderful," Pamela replied. "See you in fifteen minutes or so? I just have to pay for this." Pam gestured at the sack of cat food in her basket on the floor. Gemma hadn't even noticed her put it down.

Gemma nodded again. Suddenly she felt trepidation. What was she doing? But also lightness—she wasn't entirely alone.

As she walked out of the store, she felt her phone vibrating. She knew it was Scott. Gemma didn't even try to get the phone out of her bag in time.

As soon as it stopped ringing, she felt a pang of guilt. What if there was something up with Noah? She thought she should call back. As she found her phone, Scott called her again. This time, she answered.

He wanted to know what she was doing, where she was, when she would be home. "Why don't you come home and I'll make us some lunch?"

For a minute, Gemma thought about returning home and pretending nothing had happened. She was sure Scott would be relieved and would totally oblige—nothing being said or resolved, carry on as normal, until next time.

Was this how couples end up hating each other? All those bitter resentful women she saw daily and their completely oblivious husbands? After years together, simply codependent in their dysfunction with a blatant disregard for each other's feelings and thoughts?

Did it just start with small day-to-day things and gradually take over everything?

"That sounds great, Scott," she heard herself reply flatly. There was nothing in her voice—no life, no joy, nothing. She wondered if

Scott noticed. "I just have to do something first. I'll be back in an hour or so."

"Where are you going?" Scott sounded panicked.

"I want to check out a new thrift store in town," Gemma lied easily. "I'll see you when I get home." She ended the call before he had a chance to say anything.

Gemma walked to her car, entered Pamela's address into her navigation system, and headed that way. She felt nervous but empowered. She had somewhere to go—somewhere Scott didn't know about. It was the closest thing to running away she could bring herself to do. She knew she would not go far through. She could not leave Noah—and Gary.

Suddenly, she felt an unexpected wave of compassion sweep over her. "Father, forgive them, for they know not what they do" popped into her head, and she felt it reverberate through her bones.

Father, forgive them, for they know not what they do.

She thought she had understood the meaning behind that before (wasn't that what Jesus had cried out asking forgiveness for all those involved in his crucifixion?). Was she really asking for forgiveness here? For Scott, as well as Janine? And their selfish actions?

Gemma wasn't sure if she was ready to think about forgiveness. She was still feeling like she was being gripped at the neck while having rocks on her chest.

But with that single thought, she felt…different, but not ready to talk about it yet.

Forgiveness felt a very long way off, but still, it seemed like the right direction to face.

About ten minutes later, Gemma was pulling up to a modest home in the old established area of town. There were big old trees dripping with Spanish moss hanging over the streets and the yards, older style beach houses with sandy driveways and big yards, some neglected, some well taken care of with landscaped gardens and rocking chairs on porches that wrapped around the houses. An eclectic mix of original buildings and brand-new mansions taking up every spare foot of land, they looked somewhat too big and out of place in the old character-filled streets.

Gemma had always liked this part of town. She had been to this area a few times before, doing freelance make-up work. It had a completely different feel than the other neighborhoods—sleepy and peaceful. She liked to imagine what it must have been like even fifteen or so years ago, before the town experienced such a boom.

Pamela's was a blue and white house on stilts with a wraparound front porch and luscious leafy plants in big terracotta planters. Her white car was in the driveway, and Pamela was sitting in a wooden rocker on the porch with a jug of lemonade and two glasses.

"Hi, Gemma! So glad you found it!" Pamela beamed at her as she walked up the stairs. "Would you like some lemonade?"

It felt so nice to be seen and acknowledged. Gemma smiled back. "That would be great." She took the other rocking chair and breathed out a big sigh as she sat down.

Pamela poured her a glass and put it on the table between them. "Tough weekend, huh?"

Gemma nodded, taking a sip. The cool sweet drink tasted so good, she studied the ice cubes for a moment, unsure of what to say. She took another sip and was aware of Pamela just rocking gently looking out at the street and beyond where you could catch a glimpse of the sun sparkling on the ocean through the trees. It was nice to just sit in someone's peaceful presence. Gemma couldn't remember the last time she had experienced that.

She let out another big sigh, it came from the bottom of her soul. What was she going to do?

She took another mouthful of lemonade, letting it sit in her mouth for a moment, and then slip down her throat. Boy, it was good.

"Wow, Pamela, this is very good lemonade," she said appreciatively.

"Why thank you," she acknowledged. Then she leaned in. "I tell people it was a family recipe, but really it's just frozen from the store with the juice of a lime and some extra sugar added in." She grinned with a mischievous look on her face.

Gemma gave a surprised laugh. She had not expected that.

Pamela winked at her.

"I understand if you can't find the words yet Gemma. It's okay, you'll speak when you are ready. Are you simmering? Or on the edge of a boil right now?" Pamela asked, referring to the frying-pan analogy.

"I think I'm off." Gemma laughed in spite of herself.

Pamela laughed too.

Gemma's bag was ringing. She reached down to pull out her phone. It was Scott again. Gemma didn't answer but sent him a text. "Sorry, in the thrift store, will call when leaving."

Scott texted back. "When home? I have to work."

Nice verbiage there, Gemma thought to herself sarcastically.

Gemma looked apologetically at Pamela. "I have to call home," she offered as she stood up and made her way to the other end of the patio—out of earshot.

Pamela nodded.

Gemma called Scott's phone, she had a lump in her throat and wondered how she was going to speak.

"Hi, Gem." Scott sounded concerned. "Are you okay?"

"I'm fine." Her voice sounded wooden to her. No emotion made it to her voice—nothing. "What's up?" She tried to sound normal. But why? She sure as crap didn't feel normal, and it was his fault. Why did she feel like she had to sound like anything?

"Um, I have to go to work. The staff are falling apart. I'm just going to leave Noah here."

"What?" Gemma heard the anger in her voice. Then cynicism—"Of course, once again, put your work first over family, Scott." She spat his name. Realizing how angry she was at him, Gemma was shaking. "Just go to work then, you selfish dick. Obviously, they all mean so much more to you than your son or wife or whatever the hell lie you've been living." She snarled at him.

"Gemma, I don't have time for this right now," he stated matter-of-factly in his best GM voice. "We can talk later, okay?" She almost convinced herself that he really meant that. Or he was speaking so someone could hear him.

"Whatever." She ended the call.

By now, she was at the bottom of the stairs. Pamela was still sitting in the chair in the shade of the balcony. *She must have heard the whole thing,* Gemma thought with a pang of shame. Pamela didn't appear to have been listening; she was reading a magazine and sipping on her lemonade.

She looked at Gemma as she called up the stairs. "Pamela, I have to go and get Noah. Scott has to go to work apparently."

"Well, honey, that's fine. Why don't you bring him back and I'll make you both lunch? You must be hungry."

"Are you sure?" Gemma asked, feeling relieved. She wasn't looking forward to being across the road from Janine and her manipulative overreaching vibe. She was sure that she was milking the situation for all it was worth. Gemma didn't even want to witness that from afar.

"It's no problem at all." Pamela gave her a warm smile.

"Okay," replied Gemma, "I'll be about thirty minutes."

"Sounds great."

Gemma suddenly had the desire to have Noah with her. She didn't want him with Scott a moment longer. She was sure he probably spent the whole time lying on the couch glued to his phone anyway. Again her thoughts returned in a panic to what she was going to do.

She was in a mess for sure. She couldn't even fathom a life without or beyond Scott; however, it seemed he had envisioned life without her. *Well,* she thought stubbornly, *I'm going to have to.*

As she pulled into the street, she saw all the cars still in the driveway at Janine's house. Once again, she felt so twisted and mixed up—bad for the loss but resentful of Janine and her sly conniving ways. *She was such a shitty human being, how could Scott be so easily swayed by such a piece of trash? Wow, I really hate her,* Gemma observed. She had never experienced contempt like this towards anyone before.

As she turned in to her driveway, Scott was walking out to his car. She pulled up and wound down the window. "Would you yell out to Noah?" she asked Scott flatly.

He turned and yelled back at the house. "Noah!" He turned back toward Gemma. "Aren't you getting out of the car?"

"No, I'm good, thanks," she replied curtly.

Scott appeared not to notice. "Okay." He shrugged his shoulders.

Gemma looked away. She didn't even want to look at his face. Didn't want to meet his eyes, didn't want to let him in.

Noah appeared at the door and ran down the stairs. "Hi, Mom!" he yelled gleefully.

Gemma smiled at him. "Are you working all night?' she asked Scott, feeling the smile fall off her face.

"I don't know," he replied. "I'll call you or something."

"Sure," she answered, not believing him. She felt so sad deep down, that this man, the love of her life, now triggered the same flat emotionless tone of voice as her parents did. Wow.

Noah climbed in the backseat and did up his seatbelt. "Where are we going?"

She turned in her seat to make sure he had his seatbelt done up.

"I can do it, Mom." He swatted away her hand.

"Okay, son." She smiled at him again. She loved him so much! In that moment, Gemma knew her responsibility was toward Noah, her son. It didn't matter what Scott had done to her, it was not her job to make Scott look bad to his child. *He would be able to accomplish that all by himself,* she thought bitterly.

When she turned back, Scott was sitting in his car, looking at her. She turned her attention to the rear vision mirror. She had no desire to meet his stare. "We are going to a lady's house who is a friend from work. She is going to make us lunch."

Noah smiled again, looking excited. "Does she have any children? Or pets?"

"Her children are all grown up, honey, but she does have a cat."

Gemma had pulled out of the driveway first and glanced back down the driveway just as she was pulling away. Scott was still staring at her. She wondered if he had any feelings of remorse or regret. If he did, he wouldn't tell her. That was for sure.

How did this all go so wrong? Gemma felt the weight still on her and wondered if it would ever leave.

"Don't you think, Mom? Mom? Are you listening, Mom?"

Gemma caught Noah's tone of voice and intent gaze from the backseat, which bought her back to reality. "Honey, I'm sorry, tell me again."

"This is a good song. I know the words for this one. I want you to turn up the radio!"

Gemma gave a "Yes sir" half-salute into the rear vision mirror and turned up the radio. They spent the rest of the drive to Pamela's house singing worship songs. By the time they were pulling up to the house, Gemma felt somewhat relieved. She didn't know if that was the right word, but that was how she felt—lighter and hopeful.

Chapter 19

Change in the Wind

The afternoon was genuinely lovely. Gemma felt almost normal. It was so nice to feel like someone was happy to be with her, remember what it felt like to have a friend again. It made her realize how accustomed she was to being treated like a second-class citizen. That thought in itself made her feel angry and sad, although she realized it was her own fault too. She had accepted it and made excuses for Scott's bad behavior, always hopeful that the old Scott would be coming back.

Pamela was just the breath of fresh air Gemma had needed, the break from her current situation gave her some valuable perspective.

Gemma also appreciated that Pamela didn't needle her for details or gossip. She was just there, being a friend. They talked about cats, what Pickles liked and how often she ate. Noah told Pamela about what Gary liked to eat too and made Gemma show her the photos of Noah and Gary from her phone. They talked about Pamela's upcoming trip, when and where she would be, and the best way to contact her if needed. They ate a very European-inspired lunch of a barley and ham bone soup with crusty bread with cheese, relish, and some delicious pickles (turned out Pamela named her cat after her favorite hobby—making her own pickles and relishes).

Noah had a good time too, reading Pamela's old selection of *National Geographic* magazines from the 1980s and '90s, investigating the maps that came with them and laying on the beanbag in the sun with Pickles, the old gray cat. She was very small and bony compared to Gary their boy, but you could tell she was well loved and had a silky coat and bright green eyes.

Noah loved her instantly, burying his face in her fur. "Mom, can you hear her purring? She's so loud for being so little! Almost louder than Gary!" His brown eyes were wide with wonder. Gemma could indeed hear her purring from across the room. The atmosphere in the room was so relaxing—cat purring, late afternoon sunlight streaming across the room through the blinds. Gemma wished she could freeze the moment and halt time for a while.

Pamela let Gemma and Noah know they were more than welcome to stay at her house the whole time if they wanted. Gemma thought maybe they would stay on the weekends but reassured Pamela she would be over to see Pickles and feed her twice a day.

As they left and exchanged hugs, Gemma knew she would have the strength to go it alone and keep focused on finding the best situation for Noah and herself. Scott had evidently made his decision. He wasn't in love with her anymore. This obviously meant to him they were done. Disappointing, but it was the first time she felt she knew where she stood with him in a long time. Gemma felt more sure of herself than she had since they'd moved here.

Pretty much since they had moved to this town, when Scott got the promotion, Gemma had felt less and less like herself. But suddenly, she was back.

This was what she knew, no frills, blinders off; Scott had opted out—out of their marriage, out of being a family with her. She knew that he loved Noah—there was no question there—in his selfish, self-centered way. She also knew that God was with her. She still felt peace from the vision/dream last night. Was it a dream? It hadn't felt that way. That light and peace was real. Again, she wondered, was this what people meant when they proclaimed so loudly that Jesus had touched them? Gemma felt these were questions for analysis at another time. She just knew she felt more peace than she had for a long, long time.

Paradoxically still somewhat crushed but accepting of it, she was aware that she had stopped fighting for all of these truths she had been hanging on to—let go of the idea that Scott was her human, her partner for life, let go of the idea that she had held that she would be with him, her best friend, forever. She was surprised she was able to let go of it all. Was this what surrender felt like? She knew she had to get out of the situation. It was not good for her or Noah. She knew she needed a bigger break, a valuable change of perspective. Maybe she would just stay at Pamela's for two weeks and take advantage of the space offered. She could take Noah to school from Pamela's place just as easily, and Scott could look after Gary for a few days. They could go by every few days and check on Gary anyway. Yes, that's what she would do. Then, while she was at Pamela's, she would figure out the next step. No point in overwhelming herself now, she just had to take the next step. That's all.

Onwards.

When they got home, it was early evening. There weren't any cars at Janine's house, and Scott wasn't home at theirs.

Gemma hadn't been expecting him to be there. She'd all but given up trying to anticipate his movements now.

She'd rather not see him, although she knew she would probably have to. *Well,* she thought to herself, *I'll cross that bridge when I come to it.* Gemma was semi-impressed with her newfound patience with herself. She felt so different.

"Mom, can we watch a movie together?" Noah was kneeling on the couch, leaning over the arm with Gary sound asleep next to him.

"I need to unload the dishwasher and get some—" She caught Noah's look of disappointment and stopped herself. Why not? Why did she have to keep busy all the time? Why not just sit down with Noah and Gary on the couch and watch a movie? Even if she had seen it a dozen times. *In actual fact, that would be great,* Gemma thought to herself. *In fact, that would be the best thing I could do with myself right now.*

She smiled at Noah. "Sure, son, that's a great idea. What do you want to watch?" She already knew the answer—his all-time favorite movie ever.

He gave her his sideways smile "*The Lego Movie!*" they both said at the same time, Noah laughing.

Gemma sat down with him while he scrolled through the menu to find it. "You know, Mom," he started, still focused on the TV, "I'd like for us to stay at Miss Pamela's house and take care of Pickles."

"What about Daddy and Gary?" she replied.

"Oh, Dad would be fine, and Gary is almost always inside. It would be easy for Dad to remember to feed him," he said matter-of-factly.

Gemma felt a smile creep onto her face. "That's also a good idea!" she exclaimed. "Wow, Noah!" She put her arm around him as she settled onto the couch and pulled him in for a hug. "You have all sorts of great ideas!" She paused. "Got any more?" She ruffled his hair.

"Popcorn and ice cream for dinner?" he chirped hopefully.

Gemma laughed. She knew she had still so far to go, but she also knew she was going to be okay. She had been blessed with a wonderful little boy, and God would be with them on their journey, wherever it led.

"We'll see, honey, but right now, the odds are good."

He looked at her disbelieving. She laughed again. "Really?"

"Why not?"

Noah grabbed Gemma's face and gave her a big kiss on the cheek. "You're the *best*, Mom. I love you so much."

"I love you too, Noah." She put her arm back around him as he snuggled into place.

He looked up at her and put his finger to his lips. "*Shhh*, the movie is starting."

"Of course." Gemma nestled into the couch as well, feeling reassured by Noah's warmth and Gary's loud purrs. She didn't know what was going to happen next in their lives, but she knew she had the stamina and faith to see it through.

Yes, things were going to change.

She was at a slow simmer, and that was okay.

About the Author

With a love of travel instilled from a young age, B.A. May was born in Australia and had travelled extensively throughout south east Asia, with her sister and cabaret singer mother, before the family settled permanently in New Zealand, where she spent her formative years. This was where she discovered her love for the ocean and the great outdoors in general. As a child, she was an avid reader and would read by flashlight under the covers and tell stories to her dolls and toys and whoever else would listen.

A strong desire to do something completely different drew her away from New Zealand to the Rocky Mountains of Colorado where she met and married her husband, they remained in Vail for ten years where they were blessed by the birth of their son.

After a brief two years back in New Zealand, parental illness saw the family relocate back to the eastern United States, where she presently resides in North Carolina.

She still loves the outdoors and finds the best way to feel close to the Almighty Creator is enjoying daily walks with her dog through the woods and areas close to her home. Her favorite things to do include snowboarding in winter and spending long days on the lake with family in summer.